AUSTRALIAN SHORT STORIES

RICHARD LEE

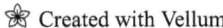 Created with Vellum

Find yourself in the natural world.

Imagine a retired writer, living in a hut in a forest beside a river in rural Australia. Drawing on memories of his life in the countryside and beside the sea and sometimes in the city, he writes stories in preparation for a time when he may forget things.

— THE AUTHOR

CONTENTS

PREFACE

AUSTRALIAN SHORT STORIES contains a variety of stories:
pastoral, political, humorous, and sometimes violent.

THE WHEEL

"Find Jack and he'll have what you want," said Andy Gorrie, stooped and peering through the open car window.

William thanked him for the map and Olive for the tea, then eased the panel van gently forward, reminding himself of the trailer behind.

As he drove through the gate, he glanced in the mirror to see Olive still standing and waving goodbye and Andy already back staring under the bonnet of one of his cattle trucks.

Andy had commented a month or so earlier, while loading stock from William's farm in the pre-dawn light, "That wagon propping up the iron shed beside your stockyards is in really good condition and it wouldn't take a lot to restore it and get it working again."

"The offside back wheel can't be rebuilt," William replied. He too had thought about bringing the wagon back to life. "Sheet of roofing iron must have come off long before I bought the place. Half the felloes are rotted and so are the spokes—and the hub is not usable. The iron tyre is good but not much use without a wheel."

There was silence but for an occasional far-off cow calling her offspring, now securely penned on Andy's truck.

A thin ribbon of light was starting to silhouette the tops of the Mountain ash on the distant ridge high above the farm, and further up the valley kookaburras called joyfully to the new day.

"Go and see Jack Jones."

"Who and where is Jack Jones?" shouted William.

Andy shone his large torch on the truck as he moved slowly around making a final check of the load which was mainly William's grass-fattened vealers.

"They should fetch top dollar," Andy muttered out loud.

An aged dairy bull and half a dozen dry dairy cows stood stoically silent in a separate pen, listening to the sounds around them. A red Dairy Shorthorn, the house cow from the Pearces' place was there too. William wondered what the Pearce kids would say when they found out that Big Red had gone; or did they already know? He had seen photos of little Rosie Pearce as a laughing baby sitting on the back of one of Red's calves being held by her father while Red licked the calf's face lovingly with her long tongue. Rosie was now in grade six at school. Perhaps they would all pile into the school bus without noticing that Red was missing from the house paddock and then be told the news at dinner that night.

Feeding a large and no longer productive cow on a small farm, especially through winter, was too costly for the Pearces' to contemplate. So was the pain of telling the six children, thought William.

Andy checked inside the truck cabin with his torch and shone it quickly on his pick-up sheet.

"That's it," he said.

Turning to William in the grey moist air, Andy relaxed into conversation mode for a moment.

"Jack Jones is the wife's uncle. He never married and lives on a block at the edge of the bush about six miles south of Lavers Hill. He must be in his late seventies. Worked most of his early life on the roads. Jack's got everything at his place. Sure to have a wheel. Talk to Olive. She'll tell you how to find him."

With that, Andy climbed into his truck, started the motor and ever so slowly moved away to the sound of stamping hooves on steel flooring.

William stood and listened as the truck sounds died away down the valley, then turned for the walk home along the narrow contour track around the hillside. Yes, he thought to himself. I will go and talk to Jack Jones.

It was mid-morning when William drove into the clearing at the front of Jack Jones's farm house. The weather was sunny and the mists that settled over the valleys each night had lifted early.

William drew up on a track that led to the back of the house. As he switched off the motor he noticed movement a hundred yards ahead, near the rim of low scrub where the forest began.

A tall figure was walking swiftly away from the house and into the forest.

Without stopping to think, William jumped from the car and called over the top of the car door in his loudest voice–the one he used at home for calling cattle down from the hills–"Jack Jones?"

The figure stopped quite still, then turned, stopped again for a moment, then slowly walked towards the car. The man was very tall and straight and as he came closer–he seemed to move in slow motion–William felt overwhelmed by his size.

"Who wants him?" growled a deep voice.

"Your niece Olive and her husband Andy said I should visit you," William said self-consciously in his best-explorer-meets-the-king-of all-these-lands voice. "My name is William and I have a wagon that is in good condition except it needs a rear offside wheel. Andy said you might be able to help me."

Jack Jones turned away slightly and stared into the forest. His hand took something from the pocket of his heavy black top coat. William saw it was a straight-stemmed smoking pipe. Jack fondled it gently, still staring into the trees.

"Five foot six or six three is it?" Jack asked suddenly.

For a moment William's mind went blank.

"Oh, five foot six inches. I brought the tyre with me if it's any help."

Jack Jones returned his pipe to its pocket, walked past William to the trailer and stared at the iron ring lying on the floor. Moments later he reached over and clutched the tyre with both hands. He held it as if he'd just found something he thought he'd lost forever.

Again there was silence. Jack stared at the tyre intently.

Just as William began to reflect on what life might be like for this man, living alone and some distance from other people, Jack Jones took off at a fast walk along the path that led to the back of the house. He said nothing and it was as if he had forgotten William, and had suddenly remembered something he had to do urgently elsewhere. He walked with great purpose, disappearing around the back of the old weatherboard.

William remained standing in the same spot for a moment. Then, just as he began to contemplate his next move, Jack reappeared, stared at him, beckoned to him to follow and again disappeared.

Behind the house the area cleared of bush was bigger than

William had anticipated. Not only that, there must have been an hectare at least, of corrugated iron and slab timber shedding set in three long lines and double-sided, not unlike horse or cattle shedding at country show grounds. The sheds were open at the front.

At first it seemed the sheds all contained ancient motor vehicles and rubber-tyred trailers–like those one saw in films set in the times between the wars–but as William followed Jack, horse drawn vehicles became more common until, in the buildings furthest away and facing south, every shed held an old wagon or dray or cart of some sort ranging from very small stylish sulkies, in which the wealthier farming families would have driven to town or to church, to huge juggernauts that were built to carry wool bales and were most likely drawn by bullock teams.

Jack had disappeared inside what looked to be a much larger shed at the end of the row. It was the only closed-in shed. William stepped through the small door after him and found himself in a vast and dimly lit workshop. It took only moments to realise this was no simple farm workshop but a complete vehicle repair shop.

William moved quietly up behind where Jack was standing. Before them, housed in a huge rough-hewn timber frame some eight foot high and thirty feet long, were wagon wheels of every size. Wagon restorer's heaven, thought William.

Jack stood with a hands on two wheels as though assessing the qualities of each one. Then he unhooked the chain that held the chosen wheel and, leaning heavily against it with his shoulder, allowed it to slowly roll forward a few inches off its ledge and free itself from the rack.

Jack stood back, still looking at the wheel, and said, "That's our baby." Then, in the same quick voice, "Cup of tea?" And he turned and headed for the bright outdoors.

. . .

Jack did not live in the house, but in a small cabin behind it. A cut-down milk churn with holes punched in the sides sat on bricks on the brick floor in the centre of the cabin. It contained a smouldering fire on which sat a blackened iron kettle.

Jack pushed dry leaves and twigs into the coals then added three blocks of wood. In a few moments a crackling fire made the dark wooden room bright and cosy.

Jack removed the lid of the kettle, lifted it off the fire and disappeared out the door, presumably to add more water.

"Do you get many people wanting help with repairs, Jack?" William asked casually when Jack returned.

Jack finished setting mugs for the tea, got some biscuits from a tin and put them on a small plate.

"I don't see people usually," he answered. His voice was low and quiet.

"I did a lot of repair work, but then the tractor come and straightaway, folk didn't want their wagons fixed. Didn't want their pulling horses any more either. Thousands of good horses suddenly disappeared off the farms and came back as fertiliser or got sent to feed city cats and dogs. The tractor changed everything."

Jack gently tamped fresh tobacco down in the pipe then got up and poured water from the kettle into the teapot. The two men sat side-on on either side of the table and facing the fire.

"I get the impression you've been here a long time, Jack," said William.

Jack reached for the teapot. He partly filled the mugs, then reached for the kettle to top-up the black brew with hot water. He placed a mug in front of William and pushed a sugar bowl and the plate of biscuits closer.

Jack drew on his pipe and settling back in his chair said, "I suppose I have."

So began an afternoon that William would remember for ever after.

Jack began to talk. William interrupted only rarely and briefly, only to clarify a point. Occasionally, while Jack talked, William reflected on his host's circumstances. Jack was born in 1900 and he was now eighty-two. He was the second youngest in a family of twelve children, two of whom were killed in the First World War.

He went to work on the roads at the age of twelve. His mother died when he was just sixteen and his father when he was nineteen.

William realised that Jack had not mentioned a wife at any time and he wondered if the man had ever been with a woman; he might never have experienced a woman's love nor a woman's wrath. Could Jack be that innocent? William wondered.

William found himself reflecting on his own life and Jack's, but there was no way to compare them. The loss of Eleanor had cast a shadow of a different colour on William's life and he often felt that he dwelt in a world quite separate from that of other people.

The holidaying couple had been driving on a country road in Bulgaria when a tractor towing a converted horse wagon swung out from a gate hidden in a high hedge. Eleanor had braked and swerved in the direction of the gate but couldn't avoid hitting the massive rear wheel of the cart. She had died instantly. People's lives can never be compared, he told himself abruptly, coming quickly back to the safety of the present.

It was now mid-afternoon and Jack, whose conversation had surpassed all of William's expectations, began to slow. It wasn't for lack of strength or will. It seemed to William that Jack was thinking deeply about something, but as yet there was no clue as to what it might be.

William suggested that maybe they could load the wheel onto the trailer and stretch their legs and Jack straight away replied, "Oh yes," tapped out his pipe and headed for the door.

He seemed to enjoy the short ride in the car down to the workshop, where together they guided the big wheel through the double doors and onto the trailer.

Jack slid a large piece of lumber under each side of the wheel to stop it rocking. Then he gave William a short discourse on what to do with the wheel when he got it back to the farm.

"The wheel is big and heavy and it's round. Make its weight and its roundness work for you when you're moving it. Don't ever put yourself in a position where you're fighting it because it will always beat you. Even if you don't get hurt, you'll surely end up feeling silly," he warned.

Then Jack pulled himself up to his full height to stretch and relax his muscles after the lifting.

Returning to the cabin, William carried in the box that Olive had sent to Jack, and after the excitement of unpacking Olive's provisions they made more tea, but this time they sipped it as they nibbled on her rich moist fruit cake.

In a little while, Jack started to talk again.

"William," he began. "I have a personal matter I wish to talk about and my observations of you suggest to me that I may discuss it freely with you and that you will be able to offer me some advice."

William thanked Jack for his kind words and said that while he would do all he could to help, he was unsure about his qualifications to do so.

"So be it," replied Jack. "Hear me out in any case. Even if you can't help me, my being able to tell someone like yourself may help me set some things right.

"I think you already know, William, I never married nor spent any time in any man and woman living together situation."

He paused and drew three fingers-full of tobacco from his tin and began to roll it around in the palm of his hand to make it ready for his pipe.

"I met a girl when I was a lad working on the new Great Ocean Road. I was sixteen and the road had only just reached Eastern View. The crew were about to push into real difficult cliff faces that would eventually get the road through to the big holiday resort town of Lorne.

"It was our monthly holiday weekend and we'd swim and play cricket on the Lorne foreshore with the local lads and in the evening we'd go to the hotel for drinks and a bit of supper and maybe a sing-a-long.

"It was there at the Grand Hotel that I first saw Kate and she saw me. She was fifteen then and the daughter of the publican, Darcy O'Malley and his wife Rose.

"We had eyes for one another the moment we met but her father noticed straight away and made sure that when us fellas came to town, Kate was kept busy with chores somewhere where she and me couldn't see each other. But sometimes, when the pub was very busy and Darcy was a bit tipsy, Kate's head would appear around a side door and she'd see me and wave and laugh before disappearing back to where she'd sneaked away from.

"Kate's mother Rose was more understanding and after a year or so and when she'd got to see that I wasn't a bad lad, she would send Kate on errands so that she could get away from the hotel for a while and we'd get to walk into town together–and in no great hurry either.

"Those times together were precious to me and I believe to her, for it was only at the end of each month when I could get there, and even then we never could be sure of getting to be alone together.

"After a year or so, the new road got close enough to the town so that we could link up with a rough timber cutter's track coming out from Lorne. At this time I got the job of driving the wagon to Lorne every Thursday, to collect the mail and bits and pieces of stores and produce that the camp may have run short of ahead of the regular shipment delivered by the boat, which called every month.

"Kate would always look out for me and sometimes she would bring me something special from the hotel kitchen. Sometimes she would laugh and tell me that I was too big for a normal wife to have to feed and look after and I'd need to marry a girl who had experience in cooking big quantities of food. A girl who had maybe worked in the kitchen of a hotel for instance. I would laugh and ask where she thought a bloke would find such a girl, then she'd yell and box my ears.

"I was very confident about my future but, for some reason, I had this feeling down deep that her father did not like me and, no matter what, would make our courtship as difficult as possible. These feelings fell away whenever I was with Kate. Being with the one you love drives away a man's worst fears, I've noticed."

Jack stopped talking for a while and refilled his pipe.

When he started again, there was a slight wobble in his voice and he stopped and coughed a bit, then started again.

"It was a month or so after Kate's seventeenth birthday and I went to Lorne to pick up extra oats and chaff for the horses and other bits and pieces. Winter had set in and the animals needed a bit more tucker each morning and night to keep them warm and working along those windy cliff faces.

"The town was quiet as I drove to the feed store. No one came out like they usually did when I pulled up. It was cold and windy and I went inside. The people working there, most of whom I knew, looked at me sort of funny if they looked at me at all. Some pretended not to see me. When I went to the counter with my list of stores, no one came to serve me. Usually they'd all say hello or yell out to ask how much road we'd dug this week.

"After a few minutes, the wife of the store owner came out to me. Old Mrs Johansson–or Florence as we were allowed to call her–was a stern woman but she was always kind to me. She somehow discovered that I had lost my mother not long before and, since then, I'd felt she took more interest in me. She never said very much but I knew she knew about me and Kate and I always felt that, behind her stern face, she liked us being together and looked out for us.

"Florence did something she had never done before. She came around from behind the counter and stood in front of me and looked directly into my face. Then she reached out and took hold of my hand and in a slow firm voice said, 'Jack, there is something I have to tell you'."

Jack stopped talking and gave another little cough. He stayed silent for a minute at least, then continued.

"I felt confused. This sort of thing had never happened when I'd come to the store before.

"Florence was dead quiet for a moment, then she said,

'Jack, the O'Malleys have gone. They left in the middle of the night three days ago and nobody knows where they went. People are saying that Darcy O'Malley had got heavily into debt gambling and, in desperation, took the family and shot through. Kate's gone, Jack. I'm so sorry."

No sound could be heard in the cabin nor from the world outside. Jack was sitting upright, a hand on each knee, and staring into the fire. He seemed not to breathe.

"It was mid-winter, as I said, and work on the road was slow due to the weather, and sometimes stopped for weeks at a time. There would be occasional slips of shale and rock to clear as cliff faces we had created, newly exposed to the weather, came down following a week or more of heavy rains and wind.

"I got time off and went to Colac first, a day's ride to the north. Then I went west to Camperdown then up and back to Ballarat, and then down to Geelong. I was away for about three weeks, which was what the boss said was all the time away he could give me. I checked every hostelry, farrier, wagon repair shop. I asked in police stations and poorhouses. I visited priests and enquired at every general store I passed. Nothing!

"A year later I placed an advertisement in the personal notices in the *Weekly Times*: Kate O'Malley–Happy birthday wherever you are. Jack Jones c/o Post Office, Lorne. I ran this advertisement on her birthday every year for at least ten years, but nothing came of it.

"Ten years passed, then early in 1931 my brother Alfred wrote to me and said I should come up to Colac for the mighty machinery sales that were to be held. These special sales had been organised to help farmers through the Depression. Alfred thought it would be an opportunity to get together and for me to maybe get a few pieces of equipment for my repair shop.

"The Great Ocean Road was completed and now ran right through to Port Campbell, but I still got paid on contract to quarry stone and gravel and maintain a big section of the road. I was doing well and had saved quite a bit of money. But I had just suffered a setback. A mismeasured fuse had set off a blast before I'd fully turned away and I'd caught a load of fine grit in the eyes. It was painful in the beginning, but became just an irritation and sometimes reduced my vision.

"A visit to a doctor in Colac was already planned for the same time as the sales. I wrote back to Alfred and said I'd see him on the first day of the sale, late in the afternoon; and, if I couldn't find him straight away, I would leave a message with the womenfolk at the Country Women's Association tent.

"Well, I got to the sale as planned. The weather wasn't the best. A dry north wind is never good for travelling. Horses don't like it. As well, I got a bit of dust in my eyes along the way which made them worse than usual.

"I came around to the northern gate of the showgrounds and furthest from the busier town side, figuring my two horses would find it quieter there and have the sun and wind behind them, once they were properly tethered."

Jack stopped for a moment and leant forward to get a lighted stick to relight his pipe. William watched in silence.

"As I went through the gate, I noticed a table under a canvas lean-to and womenfolk sitting like they were running a stall. Not seeing too well and not wanting to wipe my eyes in front of them, I walked up and asked in a friendly voice if this was the CWA booth, to which one replied that it was not but that she could point it out to me. She came around to my side of the table and standing beside me, pointed across the dusty paddock 'See the big flagpole and the big tent? Head for that and when you get to it you'll be right up close to the CWA.'

"I thanked her and without looking back, headed off in the direction her arm had pointed, squinting to see if I could find the flagpole and the big tent.

"I hadn't gone more than about thirty paces when I heard a sound coming up behind me – someone running. As I turned to see what it was, a woman who I figured was from the group I had just spoken to ran past me with both hands to her face and sobbing loudly. I tried to look back to where she had come from but could not see any sort of trouble, just the shapes of all the women standing looking towards me, or rather, at her as she disappeared. I didn't understand any of it so I went on and left my message for Alfred with the CWA women, who kept messages in a big book.

"It was early evening by the time my brother and I caught up with one another. We hadn't seen each other for almost two years and what with this huge sale and everything, there was a lot to talk about.

"Just when we'd got our animals together and sorted and fed, and as we finished our meal before laying out our bed rolls, Alfred said, 'Oh Jack. Remember that sweetheart of yours from Lorne? Well, I saw her today. I'm pretty sure it was her. I didn't try to speak to her. Only met her the once when we all came down to visit you after Mum died. Kate wasn't it? Pretty girl wasn't she? Still is. Look out for her tomorrow, Jack. I bet you'd both enjoy meeting up again.'"

The top of Jack's body swayed from side to side and he lifted first one long leg up off the floor then swapped to the other leg, all the while looking into the fire with both hands firmly clasping each knee. The movements were not those a person would make normally. William saw that it was anguish and pain like the pain and fear of a beast imprisoned in his cattle crush before marking and tagging.

After a while Jack became still again, then continued.

"I knew then who the crying woman was. I knew she didn't know that I couldn't see. Did she think I didn't recognise her or, worse, didn't want to know her? Why wouldn't she say some-thing to me. If she cared enough to cry when she saw me, couldn't she have made sure that I knew who she was?"

Jack called out these last words like a man calling for help, just as William had called out in the darkness each night for almost a year after Eleanor's death.

"And I never ever heard of her again," said Jack softly.

Neither man spoke or moved. The cabin was darker now and William suddenly felt cold. Then Jack turned from gazing into the fire and looked at William and said, this time in a clear and steady voice.

"William? I so want to see or hear from her before I die. Even if she has passed away–God forbid–I want to know where she was put to rest.

"Tell me if you can William, what should I do now?"

2

NIGHT SHIFT

I was working as a nursing aide at a large country hospital before I enrolled at university. I mostly worked night shift, and enjoyed the quietness and the lack of hustle and bustle. The work was easy, just checking on patients through the night.

Some patients were in just overnight, for minor surgery, while other more serious cases where often heavily sedated and only required their life support equipment to be monitored.

This particular night was very quiet. Only half the beds were occupied, and only one of the special care rooms contained a serious case.

Christine, the aide I was to replace, met me as usual. It was two o'clock in the morning and she said everything was under control and the patients were all sleeping comfortably.

Then Christine took me to the special care room, and we stood outside while she gave me the details of the case, and what we were expected to do. She said that Matron had indi-cated that, at the moment, it was unclear whether the special care patient would last through the night.

Christine explained that the man had been brought in unconscious, having survived a very nasty motorbike accident coming through the mountain pass to the north of the town. He was now on life support, but it was also important to keep his temperature down. For that reason, staff were asked to spend a little time every hour or so swabbing his body with a sponge and cold water.

Now that Christine had outlined the duties for my shift, she took me in to see the patient.

The man was huge and he was hairy, and probably in his late thirties. His eyes were closed and he was eerily silent. Only a single dial beside the bed confirmed that he was breathing. He lay naked, but for a sheet covering his lower half.

I thanked Christine and she prepared to leave; then she stopped and turned and looked at me and smiled, and in a hushed voice, provided a final piece of information.

"Just one other thing I should tell you Freya. He has tattoos, as do most of the bikie patients we get admitted. But he does have a special one."

I asked Christine what was special about it.

"He has a honey bee tattooed on the end of his penis. One of the day staff said that when he first came in he had a partial erection, probably caused by a rush of adrenalin or a sudden hormone surge in the moments leading up to the accident. She said that the bee had its wings extended, but later, when the erection subsided, it appeared to have them folded."

I was looking at her in amazement and Christine laughed.

"Thought I should tell you just in case you thought it was a real one and started madly beating him with a fly swat."

We both laughed nervously, then she left me to it.

I shut the door behind her and turned to look at my patient. He looked so gentle, so serene. His long blond hair and strong square chin made him look like a sleeping Viking chieftain, the sort we might see in a movie or picture book. His huge muscular arms could have easily swung a sword to cut off his rival's head and limbs. They rested beside his body and his giant open hands faced upward.

I lifted the patient record sheet from the end of the bed and read his name Odin Amundsen. Definitely a Viking, I mused. His ancestors might easily have known mine way back when so many girls would have been named Freya.

I collected a sponge and a bowl of water and started the task of keeping the giant cool. I began with his brow, face and neck. His skin was taut and leathery. One could have been wiping down a leather skirt, or a snakeskin handbag.

As I prepared to move to his chest, I had a sudden desire to kiss Odin, so I leant forward and lightly touched his lips with mine. But then I wanted more, and pushed my mouth harder against his lips. It gave me a beautiful feeling, and I suddenly felt very happy.

I sponged his broad shoulders with one hand while I burrowed my fingernails into the forest of hair on his chest. Swabbing Odin was suddenly feeling exciting, and I began to concentrate on each moment with loving attention.

I had not had a lot of experience with men. I probably should say I'd had none. As I grew older I began to realise that being so tall and thin, and being flat chested, I wasn't going to get men rushing to me with offers of a romantic date, or with bunches of flower or chocolates.

As I said, I experienced a growing feeling of excitement as I swabbed Odin. I began to have thoughts about things I could do, quite inappropriate things, and that made me more excited.

I went back to Odin's face and kissed him again. I even ran

my tongue across his closed lips. Then I moved back down, just below his chest where the long hair stopped and his shorter belly hair began. I looked at his hand lying beside him, and only inches from the edge of the bed and where I stood. His bed was quite high but because I'm tall, it didn't seem unduly so.

I reached out and slid my hand beneath his, and lifted it. I had a sudden thought; I can have his hand if I want to. I looked at his long thick fingers. For all I knew–or rather didn't know–about men's penises, any one of Odin's fingers looked capable of doing what a penis did.

With my other hand, I lifted up the hem of my nurse uniform exposing my panties. Then I took Odin's hand and placed it between my legs and rocked it slowly to and fro. Then I took hold of his index finger, pulled my panty crotch to one side and placed the tip of his finger against my wet pussy. It felt wonderful. But then I remembered the story of the bee and I put his hand back and went and drew back the sheet, all the way to the bed end.

Probably through lack of experience, I've never thought a lot about the size of men's penises. Odin's penis looked very large, even though it was resting, and at its base was a coconut-sized bunch of testicles nestled inside a mass of blond hair. And sure enough, there was the honey bee neatly tattooed on the big reddish brown bulb at the top of his penis which stood up through this nest of blond hair.

Looking at his manhood was so invigorating and I desperately wanted to have it, to own it.

I wriggled my hand down into the hair to find the base of his penis and when I did, I clasped it tightly and closed my eyes. I found myself shaking just a little, but didn't know why.

And now I knew what I most wanted to do in the whole

world. I still had an hour before I was to be relieved for my tea break. I locked the door.

I had entered a state of being that I did not understand, but did not want to stop. I removed every piece of clothing and footwear. Then I climbed up onto Odin and flattened and pressed my body against his. I felt so calm, and what began as excitement, morphed into a sort of ecstasy and I sighed and shut my eyes.

I must have lain there for a good ten or fifteen minutes, most happy with my lot. I thought how nice it was to lie on top of a person. In fact, to this day lying on someone is one of my favourite loving positions, even if fully dressed and not feeling especially sexual.

Some time had passed and I was feeling sleepy; then I imagined I felt something between my legs. I managed to not flinch or respond. Yes, something was definitely moving slowly up between the top of my thighs, pushing my flesh gently aside as it did so.

I was mesmerised. I couldn't move. I didn't want to move. I wanted whatever it was to keep coming up towards my crotch.

So much rushed through my mind. I couldn't take it all in. I lifted my head slowly, and opened my eyes and looked at Odin's face, but nothing about it had changed.

Then without planning to do so, I found myself moving my legs apart, and edging down to meet whatever it was, coming up towards me.

I had already felt a tiny orgasm and I knew that I was wet, and getting wetter. Suddenly, whatever it was pushed against my vagina, and I opened like a flower and spread my wetness everywhere.

I now knew exactly what was happening and I didn't want it to stop. I started to move down again and as I did so, I opened up and sucked in Odin's penis head, but I kept on moving down along his huge shaft. Further and further down I wriggled, and Odin came further and further up into me.

I began to sob. I wanted Odin to put his giant arms around me and fasten me permanently to his body. I wanted to run my hands through his long hair and stick my tongue into his mouth. I wanted him fully alive.

I stopped crying, settled down and rode my Viking's manhood like I was riding a galloping horse. I desperately wanted to feel him come inside me, and he did.

At first he frightened me with his bellowing roar. But he only roared once, when he sent a torrent of sperm into my helplessly lustful little vagina.

I heard myself calling out, "Yes Odin, yes!"

I lay still for a long time but all was quiet. Odin didn't move or make another sound. I heard a bell ringing in the distance, and knew that my time was up and that someone would be looking for me. I dragged myself off my Viking lover and stood up.

I looked at his penis, still standing tall, sticking out of its luxuriant blond nest. And there was the honey bee, wings spread wide, and drinking from the hole in Odin's penis.

I quickly cleaned Odin, swabbed his belly and pulled the sheet back over him. Then there was a knock on the door and I called "Coming, just give me a moment please."

I threw on my clothes and headed out the door.

"How is he?" asked the lass who had looked after him the night before.

"Nothing seems to have changed," I answered, trying not to look at her and thinking that I must look dreadful.

"He can't last much longer. He just didn't seem to want to go. Like he was waiting for something," said the nurse.

I stared at her.

"Do you believe he will die?"

"The doctors and surgeons think so. It's a brain problem. It's no longer connected to his body, or something."

I turned abruptly and hurried away, unable to get my mind around it all. Had I simply imagined everything? Had it not really happened? But what was leaking from me now was proof that something had happened, something beautiful and amazing.

I got to work early the next night. I'd spent the whole day wondering and daydreaming. Dreaming that Odin would recover and throw me on the back of his big motorbike and we'd ride off into the distance. But that was not to be.

"They found him dead early this morning. Strange though! He had his one good eye open, and a most angelic smile on his face," said a nurse going off duty.

"And the girl that found him said he had an amazing erection and that the bee tattoo was truly beautiful."

When my night shift finished, I went to Odin's room. It was not occupied so I sneaked in and locked the door and lay on the bed and cried and cried, and I imagined that I was the wife of an ancient Viking god.

3

PIZZA

The motor gave a couple of unhealthy grunts when Rod switched off the ignition of the old Land Cruiser, reminding him he must buy oil soon.

Tonight's campsite was much like those of the past week, though the landscape here was not so dry or sparse. A wide expanse of good grass beside the narrow ribbon of road, and a nearby creek would provide grazing and water for the horse.

Rod let down the back of the float and backed Betty out onto the soft grass. The fine animal threw up her head and shook her strong neck, then pawed the ground in front of her in anticipation. She was happy to be let out, and keen to move her large and muscular body.

"Easy girl," Rod murmured.

Betty snorted and threw up her head again, pleased to be free of the confinement and those long hours in the float.

Rod led her down to a cleared spot beside the creek where drovers watered their stock. The Warmblood mare stood quite still at the edge of the water and moved her head one way then the other, her ears pricked and forward to catch any sounds, while her nostrils flared and twitched as she sampled the fresh new smells. In her whole life, she had never experienced danger when drinking, but her primeval instinct demanded she check thoroughly before drawing in the clear water now cooling her front hooves.

Leaving the creek, Rod walked and trotted the horse along the roadside for a kilometre before tethering her for the night. He would ride her for half an hour at sun-up before moving on. Betty again stood motionless, listening and smelling the air. Then she walked away from Rod, head down, looking for just that right spot in the sweet grass to begin the night's grazing.

Rod connected the outside light, lit the small kero stove and put a saucepan of water on to boil. He peeled three potatoes and a carrot, then rummaged through the big wooden box which was his larder and found a piece of hard cheese hiding in a brown paper bag, and a tin of sardines he didn't know he had. That's a bonus, he thought, and reminded himself that tomorrow morning early would be the best time to catch a bunny or hare, or maybe a duck at the creek.

Rod had quit his job in Ceduna in South Australia a week before and headed off intending first to visit his old mum in Rupunyup, just north of the Grampians, then on to his older brother Angus's farm, farther up at Wedderburn, where he hoped to be able to leave the horse while he sought out and negotiated with Warmblood breeders to find a suitable sire to join her with. The stud fee was going to be high and he needed to have enough money saved by the end of September. He figured he would go on to Melbourne and find work for a few months, most likely as a security guard with an armoured car company. He had experience and good references from previous stints in the city. Then he would go bush again.

Rod's plans for Betty had been brought forward a year and without warning. Breaking up with Annie had been sudden, and just as he had done at the time of previous break-ups, he loaded the truck and moved on.

Rod was good-looking–if unusually gaunt,–and tall and lean. Born on a farm and the youngest of seven, he had learnt to break in horses by the time he was sixteen. At eighteen he had taken a teacher training course and become a young schoolmaster in a one-teacher bush school. But the ladies loved him and too often, against anyone's better judgement except his own, he loved them back. That they often already had a partner meant that Rod's life could become suddenly far too complicated and even uncomfortable.

But it was Rod's rare qualities, his speed and style and bravado that combined and made him different from most men and it usually meant that he could rarely stay in one place for very long before finding himself either constrained or unwelcome. He learnt early in his working life how to live alone and, more often than not, on the move.

It wasn't that Rod was a bad person–far from it. He had the proverbial heart of gold. He was just too good at inspiring people. His country boy agility and enthusiasm mesmerised people and swept everyone along in a world that, on their own, they could never sustain. Women queued to dance with him at country balls. Looking like a gentleman from a period movie in his tuxedo, bow tie and shiny pumps, he carried each one of them around the dance floor with a style so exhilarating that they most likely never experienced anything like it again; and they talked about it among themselves for months afterwards.

To Rod, life was as straight forward as taking a horse over

a jump or a creek. "A horse doesn't jump of its own accord," he would say in a loud voice, laughing and with merriment in his eyes. "You lift a horse over a jump with your mind. If you didn't, you'd both end up on the ground. If you don't know where you're going, don't expect the horse to know."

Tonight, Rod was feeling just a tad more tired than usual and more hungry. He thought how he'd love a bath and a shave, and maybe a large pizza with the lot and even to sleep in a proper bed with a mattress. He was still a couple of days away from Rupunyup. He had chosen to come the long way using back roads. It wasn't that he was in trouble or anyone was looking for him, he simply wanted to be alone, and he liked to see the country away from the main highways. A young Australian Greek bloke had given him a well-worn map of South Australia and Western Victoria on which was marked the zigzag route taken by men who carried illegal undersized shark from fishermen in the Spencer Gulf to the fish and chip loving Melbournites. It went through a lot of country Rod had never seen.

Rod had just dropped the potatoes in to cook when Betty gave two short snorts. Rod straightened up and listened, and saw far-off headlights coming from the direction he would be taking next day. He knew he wasn't far from the small town of Bunneringee so it was more likely he would see somebody go past here than in the bigger, more empty country he'd recently passed through. A farmer going home probably-or maybe a refrigerated van on it's way to fetch illegal fish?' he mused.

Five minutes later the vehicle slowed as it drew closer. The small light in his truck had been noticed, even though it was parked some distance from the road. Rod instantly ran through the short checklist of the things he always thought about when his space might be invaded: friend or foe, police or hoons, (no such thing as one hoon or even two; cowards always travel with at least two other cowards), everything legal…rifle locked in thief–proof metal trunk and with firing pin removed…truck registration paid up…tyres and muffler OK and so on.

The car passed slowly by and, as it did so, a beam of light bathed Rod and his campsite. It made a slow turn, and drove off the road and pulled up thirty metres behind the float.

Police; act a bit dumb,' Rod told himself gently. He tuned his brain down to placid and not street wise; easier for everyone, he thought.

The spotlight went off and two doors opened and closed simultaneously, and the occupants came over to where Rod stood looking towards them.

"G'day," he called out in an even and friendly voice.

"G'day," came back a young and uncertain reply.

Two young constables came into the light, each one looked about. One walked around to the front of the Land Cruiser to check the rego sticker while the other shone his torch into the back of the open truck. Rod could see they were very young and something told him they might not be from the country, though he couldn't be sure. Who knows these days, he thought, the cities are reaching right out to the bush. These two were probably drinking cappuccinos in Bunneringee twenty minutes ago.

The constable who looked and sounded the eldest turned to Rod and said, "Where are you from?"

Rod thought quickly. He didn't want to get caught up in long explanations about himself. It was probably better to stick with the truth for the time being. More likely than not, they wouldn't check him out once they saw he had nothing to hide. For the moment though, he might not tell them exactly where he was headed, just to protect his old mum from any "routine enquiries" if anything went wrong.

"I came from Penola today," Rod replied, "but started out a week ago from Ceduna." His tone was open and matter–of–fact.

The constables seemed unsure of what to do next. There didn't appear to be anything suspicious with this man's lonely campsite, ten kilometres out of town. They could ask him a lot of tricky questions, even search his truck for drugs, but his relaxed and genial manner didn't draw them in that direction. Just as it looked as if they might quietly leave, a loud cough came out of the darkness. Both men turned instantly towards it and as one, shone their torches on Betty, now at the far end of her long rope, happily wrenching large mouthfuls of sweet grass from the ground.

The two men walked slowly forward towards the horse and Rod followed.

Rod felt a sudden tension. The young men exchanged glances then both looked at Rod. "Do you have a receipt or other proof of ownership for that horse?" the older one asked in a police academy official tone. Before Rod could answer, the younger of the two blurted out enthusiastically, "It's the missing horse all right. The report said a grey gelding with dark points. I remember because Janice in the office said they were not common. She keeps horses so she'd know. Oh, and the dark points are the tail, and the long hair on the neck, the mane–just like this one."

"Well?" said the other constable. "Can you prove ownership?"

Rod had listened carefully to what the younger man had said. He turned things over in his mind with bemused and growing interest then answered, "To be honest, I can't right now. Mind you, I don't think many people with horses could prove ownership very easily on such short notice as this."

"You must have someone who could vouch for you being the owner," replied the policeman.

It was then that Rod decided his sudden hunch to go down an as yet unmapped track had been worth the risk. He quietened himself inside before answering.

"No, I can't easily find someone, especially at this time of night. But that doesn't mean the horse isn't mine, surely?" A tiny hint of challenge crept into his voice.

"We'll have to follow this up," said the constable. "I'll have to ask you to pack up and follow us to the station."

Rod thought quickly, then said, "Isn't it a bit late constable? I could come in early tomorrow and we could sort it out then."

"Can't do that. Be too hard to explain to the sergeant if you didn't show up. And if you can't explain, then you're in a bit of trouble anyway."

Rod thought for a moment, then said, "I can't see how I can prove ownership this late in the day, so I guess you will have to hold me or the horse or both until tomorrow. Am I right?"

"Both. Otherwise we might be left with a horse but no suspect," replied the constable.

"Or a suspect and no horse if somebody came here and stole it during the night," added the enthusiastic younger constable.

"Well, where will you put us both?" asked Rod innocently.

"You can sleep in the lockup, its very comfortable. And there's a paddock behind the station where the ranger puts stray stock."

Rod said "OK. But I'm not a horse thief. I know you

blokes are only doing your job, so it's OK with me. Give me a few minutes to put the horse in the float."

Rod emptied out the water and the now soggy potatoes, and loaded his cooking gear into the truck. Then he got his own torch from the cabin, brought Betty back to the float and loaded her carefully, thinking as he did so that this old float might not be big enough if he had to move Betty when she was eight or more months pregnant.

The policemen had returned to their car to wait, putting on the spotlight so that Rod could see to make the float and back of the truck secure. When he was done, he waved and climbed in the cabin and started the motor.

The ride into Bunneringee didn't take very long, and the police car led him round to the back of the station where there was a large car park and a gate leading into the police paddock.

The older constable told Rod to come in as soon as possible, and left the younger constable to watch over the proceedings. Rod opened the gate of the small paddock and walked in a few paces to see where Betty would be for the night. Streetlights on one side allowed him to check that the fences were high enough to let her run free and not be tethered. She would like that. The grass looked reasonable and there was no indication that other stock had been in there recently.

"Everything all right?" asked the young constable.

"Yes," said Rod. "Just need to check the water trough," he called over his shoulder as he walked to the concrete trough on the fence away from the road. He cupped his hand and scooped up water, lifting it to his nose to smell it, then he tasted it to check that it was fresh and drinkable.

After Betty had been put away, Rod collected his bag and followed the constable into the station through the back door.

The older constable, Constable Blake as Rod discovered a

few minutes later, had just completed some paperwork. He turned as they came in, saying, "Rodney Drummond, I've made out my report up to this point. If you are willing to remain here overnight, we can finish the inquiry in the morning when the day shift arrives. If you feel you need to contact a solicitor or ask someone to contact a solicitor on your behalf, you are free to use the telephone. If you wish, I can supply you with the names and numbers of solicitors in the district. It's up to you."

Rod thought how nice these lads were. Good job I'm not a hardened criminal, he thought. To the constables he said, "If it's all right with you, I've had a long day and I'd prefer to leave all that until the morning."

"OK. Constable Anderson will show you to the lockup just down the passage. If you would give me the keys of the truck and your driver's licence to hold overnight, you are free to move around the station except behind the counter here in this office. You will find a bathroom with all facilities–shower, bath, toilet–at the end of the passage, and the canteen is through the door before your cell door. Any questions?" asked Constable Blake.

Rod quietly thanked them both while he searched for his keys and licence. Then he said, "I'm very hungry. I was making dinner when you arrived. I haven't eaten since early this morning and I don't have much food on the truck. I've got a few dollars on me. Can I send out for something or is it too late?"

Constable Blake looked up at the wall clock above the counter, then at Rod. "Is a pizza OK? We have to give you a meal and that's about the best we can offer, so what would you like on it?"

Rod blessed his luck and smiled inside. A little film showing him lifting a horse over a jump, played on his screen and he said, "Can I have a large pizza with the lot please?"

The policeman lifted the telephone, jabbed a button and said almost immediately, "Hi! Harry? Constable Blake. Yes I know we've already eaten, Harry. We've got a visitor. Yes Harry, just one. Yes Harry, we know you want us to lock up a whole bus load. Harry. Just send us a large pizza with the lot. OK? Oh, and hang on." He put his hand on the mouthpiece and looked back up at Rod. "Would you like an apple turnover or banana fritters with that?"

"An apple turnover would be perfect," Rod replied, smiling dreamily.

"And an apple turnover, Harry. Twenty minutes? OK. Thanks."

"OK, Rodney Drummond. Food will be here in about twenty minutes. Why don't you go and sort your bed out and make yourself comfortable. Help yourself to tea or coffee," said Constable Blake, turning back to his paperwork.

"There's also Milo," added Constable Anderson cheerily.

Rod beamed at him as the young man turned to show him the way. I love these guys, he thought.

Waking up early had never been difficult for Rodney, but this morning was a little unusual. The hot bath, shampoo and shave; the pizza 'with the lot' followed by the apple turnover and washed down with a mug of Milo combined with a comfortable mattress and a soft pillow kept him from jumping up in his usual fashion.

When Rodney did open his eyes, his first thought was that he was still dreaming. An attractive woman in police uniform was standing in the cell doorway. She was writing on a clipboard and it was a moment or two before she noticed him looking at her.

Sergeant Elaine McKenna stared back at Rod and said in a low firm voice, "Perhaps you'd like to think about getting up soon. Your mare is a little concerned about you." Then she left the room, leaving the door wide open to the passage.

Rod heard her walk back down towards the office, then loudly ask someone, "Are those two still here? Send them in would you. Yes, I know they've knocked off but I want to see them now, pronto." A door banged somewhere down in the same direction.

Rod lay still for a few minutes, too comfortable to get up. Then he rose and dressed and put his things into his bag and put it beside the open doorway. He went to the bathroom and splashed cold water on his face, then peered through the small louvre window. Betty was standing at the gate. A young woman was rubbing her muzzle and patting her neck. Janice from the office, thought Rod.

Rod ambled down to the office counter. As he arrived, a door opened nearby and Constables Blake and Anderson came out. Both looked uncomfortable. Behind them, through the open door, he saw the Sergeant behind a desk, her face still as it was, not quite severe but definitely serious, tight lips and "don't touch me" eyes. Still attractive, he thought.

"Good morning," said Rod. He would have beamed his biggest smile, but circumstances told him this was not appropriate. Instead, he offered a sympathetic grin.

"Why didn't you say the horse was a mare?" growled Constable Blake.

"Yeah. How were we to know it wasn't a gelding?" asked Constable Anderson.

Rod felt sort of sorry for the two, but it was hard to stop himself laughing out loud.

"Well fellas, firstly, you didn't ask me if the horse was a gelding, and secondly, if you had and I'd have said, 'No it was a mare', would you have believed me? And if neither of you could tell the difference anyway, how could I have proved to you that it wasn't a gelding?"

The two looked at Rodney for a moment then turned and left. Rod leant on the counter and watched them leave, happy that he had played a part in their education.

Sergeant McKenna came out of her office and went behind the counter. She said nothing as she handed Rodney his keys and licence. Silently, she put a form detailing the return of his possessions on the counter in front of him and held a pen out to him for his signature.

Rod signed the form, put his keys in his pocket and slipped his licence into its place in his wallet. His movements were particular and measured, just as they were when he saddled a horse. Then he looked at the sergeant. He met her steady gaze and, for the first time since arriving at the station, he was himself. He allowed her to see into his eyes and who he really was. Not that it mattered particularly, but she had a presence, which he recognised. He could tell she was one of the people you come across occasionally; people who knew things. He never hid himself when in the presence of this sort of person; unless the person was bent, that is, or deception was essential for survival.

"Thank you," said Rod, with a gentle smile.

"That's OK," she replied. Then she smiled, and for a moment he thought he saw who was really behind the mask, but Constable McKenna didn't let him in and he liked her the more for that.

Rod collected his bag and left through the back door.

Betty called out excitedly when he appeared, and the young woman standing near her looked up at him.

"What's her name?"

"Betty," said Rod leaning forward as the mare pushed her great head against his chest as if she were admonishing him for being late up.

"Will you breed with her soon?" asked the girl.

"Yes. I'm just starting to look for a good stallion. Hopefully, I'll find one soon if she's to be mated this season."

Janice looked up at Rod, then she pulled a small card from the pocket of her parka and offered it to him.

"Sergeant McKenna said I could give you her card but only if you wanted it. She breeds Warmbloods. Has a stud with her brother a few miles out of town. She fell in love with your mare as soon as she saw her. Checked her out as soon as she arrived at work this morning. Said she should be put in foal this year. Do you want it?"

Rod blinked and rolled the movie back to the inscrutable sergeant. Then he thought about Betty and getting her in foal, and about the difficulty he might have finding the right stallion. And there was always the chance that he had left it too late and the stallion would be fully booked, and he'd be told to put her name down for next season.

Then in his mind's eye, Rod saw a horse being taken over a jump, just as he always did when special or difficult things were working out the way he thought they should, but this time, the rider wasn't him; it was a woman. A smile crossed his bony face and he let out a deep and relaxed sigh.

Rod looked down at the young woman still holding out the card towards him. "Yes Janice, I would like it. Thank you," he said softly.

4

KNOCKOUT

When Paul found the boxing tent he couldn't have been more surprised.

A large sign announced that the celebrity middleweight Fritz Holland, from America, would be the star performer and that a purse of ten pounds was offered to anyone who could last a full three rounds with the great man. Paul had seen his boxing hero, Les Darcy, fight and beat this man at the West Melbourne Stadium five years earlier, after losing to him in Sydney the year before. It was a match Paul would never forget. What luck it would be for him to get into the ring with Fritz Holland.

Paul headed to the butcher's stockyards on the edge of town where he and Jack and two other young workers from the Ocean Road gang were camped for the weekend. The hot sun was tempered by a south-westerly sea breeze and the silence of the bush was broken only by flocks of noisy lorikeets.

Paul pitched a fork-load of hay to the horses from the lean-to at the end of the bunkhouse, then he went in and rolled out his swag and lay down. It was cool inside and the sea breeze and the shade from the trees provided the perfect spot for an afternoon nap.

It was nearly time for Kate O'Malley to go back to work. She and Paul's mate Jack sat on the bench overlooking the sea beside the path which led up to her family's hotel. As they chatted, Kate's older sister Anna walked down towards them on her way into town. She carried a small suitcase and a shopping bag.

"Hello Kate. Mum's all sorted for the evening and Dad's in a good mood. Well, sort of. He usually gets grumpy when I have a Saturday night at Edna's but he didn't seem so bad this afternoon. Hi, Jack. Tell me, what is your good-looking friend Paul, doing tonight?"

"Hello Anna. When I called for him early yesterday morning, I saw him slip his boxing gloves into his kit. I can't think of any reason for him to bring them to town other than that the carnival down on the foreshore might have a boxing tent. If that is the case, he certainly would be there."

Both Anna and Kate looked at Jack in disbelief. Anna spoke first.

"You're kidding us aren't you? Paul a boxer? He's not the type, surely?"

Jack laughed.

"If there is a boxing tent at the carnival, I'm sure that's where you will find him. Oh, but don't tell him I told you. He likes to keep it a secret. Paul thinks most people don't understand boxing, so he firmly believes that it is best they don't know about it."

Jack stood and took Kate's hand and pulled her up from the seat.

Anna looked at the couple and laughed.

"You two look more like an old married couple every day. Thanks, Jack. Maybe I'll look out for him if I get to the carnival. Bye."

Kate watched as her sister walked gracefully down the hill, looking elegant and stylish as always, even though she wore only a summer frock and sandals.

"When my beautiful sister dresses up in what she has hidden in that little overnight case and puts on her make-up, no man will be able to resist her. Paul doesn't stand a chance if Anna decides she wants him," Kate said with a knowing smile.

Jack looked at Kate and rolled his eyes and laughed.

Paul carried a small army shoulder bag containing his boxing gloves, a hand towel and a clean shirt. It would also be where he put his penknife and money and the other things from his pockets before he got into the ring. When he reached the town Paul went down to the beach and splashed his face, wetted and rubbed his hair; and washed his hands. He was ready.

Anna had just finished putting on her make-up after first sliding into a tight dress, stockings and heels when the girls knocked on Edna's front door. Gladys and Alwyn came in like excited children squabbling on their way to a picnic.

"You do what you like but I'm going to see the film," said Alwyn emphatically.

"We always do what you want to do. I want to go to the fair," replied Gladys.

Anna listened to the two and smiled.

"What do you want to do, Anna?" asked Gladys.

"Well, I've got a bit of a headache and I won't be much fun, so I'm going to have an early night. I won't go to the pictures but I'm happy to take a walk around the fairground. Why don't we do that now, then you two can still catch the late showing. What do you think?"

"All right, let's do that. Happy now Gladys? You might get to see the American boxer you keep on about. You haven't stopped talking about him since you read about him in the paper," said Alwyn. "I hope you won't be disappointed. He might not be the turn-on you expect."

"What he does in the ring will be the turn-on," said a smiling, older and wiser Gladys. "You two can keep your pretty boys. I know what matters." They all laughed.

A short fat man with a deep gravelly voice and a megaphone yelled out "Fritz Holland!" and turned to welcome the American as he climbed through the ropes. People booed and cheered and yelled out as the man in the bright red dressing gown stood grinning in the middle of the ring.

Holding his arm up to ask for quiet, the tubby spruiker paused, then spoke.

"Today we have the privilege of witnessing the talents of one of America's foremost middleweight boxers. Fritz Holland so liked Australia that he decided to come back and see more of the country."

He turned and nodded towards the boxer.

"Thank you, Fritz. Is there anything you would like to say to the audience?"

The boxer smiled back, then turned and scanned the people watching.

"We are here to see boxing at its best. Mr Lester Hammer here, my promoter, has made this possible. I cannot box without a partner so all we need now is for one of you Aussie lads to step up and show us what you're made of."

With that, he stood back and rotated slowly, waving majestically to the crowd.

"All right, ladies and gentlemen. You know the rules. They are pretty simple. If a challenger lasts three rounds with our man or counts out, he collects ten pounds. So who do we have? Who is here tonight who dares challenge our American friend? Come forward and make yourself known now. You could walk away with ten pounds or at least the honour of knowing that you had the courage to get into the ring with the famous Fritz Holland. Come on lads. How about it?"

The crowd yelled and laughed and men slapped each other on the back and urged one another to step up.

Paul put up his hand and moved forward. Within moments he was in the ring. An attendant took his details, then stepped quickly over to Lester Hammer and whispered in his ear. Paul removed his shirt, then took his gloves out of the bag and handed them to a man named Rod who was to act as his second.

"Put your hands together and welcome our challenger, local boy Mr Paul Stoner."

Rod adjusted and laced Paul's gloves, then smiled pleasantly and said, "Best of luck, mate!"

Paul waved to the crowd. Then, from the corner of the ring, he watched and waited for the referee's instructions, running slowly on the spot to loosen up.

Paul watched Fritz Holland remove his robe and limber up. He reminded himself that they were not fighting in a proper boxing match. If Fritz Holland were to fight in a proper tournament, he would have studied his opponent to plan his strategy. This situation was very different.

Fritz only had to beat up hard on the opponent, knowing

that they were unlikely to survive his attack. And he knew that he had to go easy to start with, to let his opponent get to the end of the second round or, ideally, just into the third round so that the audience felt they had got their money's worth.

Paul wondered what Fritz was doing here anyway. No one comes back to see the countryside and work for next to nothing when they have been used to earning more than a year's pay for just one fight. Paul figured that something must have gone terribly wrong for the legendary Fritz Holland, back in America.

It was then that Paul noticed that, although Fritz was looking around and grimacing menacingly and shouting at the crowd, his eyes seemed unfocused. No doubt he could still see a man shaping up to him in the ring, but how clearly, Paul could not tell.

If Paul was right, Fritz only had to keep attacking whatever was in front of him long enough to keep that person on the run or until he cornered him and dropped him to the floor. And it was only three rounds of three-minutes.

Paul had always thought that Fritz Holland must have tricked Les Darcy into committing the foul that lost Les the fight in Sydney in 1914, although he failed to work out how Fritz would have done this. Avenging his now dead hero, if he succeeded, would be a hollow victory against a handicapped man. Paul would need to work things out as he fought.

The referee called the two men into the centre of the ring, muttered the usual words about understanding the rules of the contest and got the pair to shake hands and return to their corners. As Paul continued to limber up, Rod leant over the ropes and whispered to Paul.

"He'll come out like a bull."

When the bell rang, Fritz did just that. Hardly had Paul moved than Fritz was at him with rapid punches, driving him back towards the ropes. Paul had wanted to give the impression that he was a rookie with foolhardy courage and no boxing acumen, but he was forced to react defensively and professionally, very quickly.

When he ducked down and landed a straight left to Fritz's solar plexus, his opponent immediately understood that Paul was a boxer. Fritz slowed, looking more intently at Paul while constantly edging forward, keeping up the pressure on his young opponent.

Paul could see that Fritz was slightly taller than himself, and estimated he was carrying more weight. It meant that Fritz was not as fast on his feet and that would be to Paul's advantage. Agility and lightning reflexes were essential for a successful defence when under extreme pressure.

Occasionally, Fritz would lunge forward in an effort to get in close. His constant left hooks and jabbing were easy to avoid. His close-quarter punches—delivered in rapid succession and in a variety of combinations—never found their mark.

Paul twice repeated his ducking and straight right to the solar plexus, but although his punches were powerful, on their own they would not achieve much. For the moment though, Fritz had no idea what Paul might be capable of.

Then Paul made a mistake. From his basic stance position, Fritz suddenly waved his left elbow up and down five or six times, like a chook flapping a wing. If it had been only once or twice, Paul would have dismissed it as simply a flexing to adjust a muscle position. In the moment it took to run Fritz's action through his catalogue of known moves it was too late. The straight right to Paul's chin knocked him backward with such force that he hit the ropes.

Paul immediately bounced forward back towards his

opponent. Fritz was waiting for him with another punch to the side of the head. Paul reeled back to the ropes again. Bringing all his senses to bear, he ducked to the left of the oncoming boxer who bounced back from the ropes, turning to face him as he did so.

Paul was there waiting for him. Bent low and coiled, he came to life with a left and a right and another straight left before Fritz Holland could steady himself to fight back. Fritz fell to his knees; then he was back up and looking for Paul. The crowd was becoming excited.

The bell sounded and the two fighters went to their corners. Paul appreciated the water Rod poured on his head. It was hot outside and doubly so in the tent.

"You're good, so he'll try to finish you in the next round. He won't want a third. Best of luck."

Rod swabbed Paul's forehead and neck with the cold wet towel as the bell sounded for the second round.

Paul had decided to take the initiative and lead the fight. It seemed Fritz had the same idea, coming out determined to put Paul away for good.

Paul had underestimated his own strength. At the end of that first round, he realised he could deliver punishment equal to anything that Fritz Holland could manage.

While Paul knew that leading the fight was fraught with dangers, it made sense that he should step up to the challenge. He wanted to look back on this encounter with pride. Simply surviving it would never be enough.

They came together immediately. Fritz threw his most powerful straight left which, if it had connected, would have dropped Paul to the floor. Paul blocked Fritz's left with his right glove and returned his own straight left to Fritz's chin. It was Fritz's second visit to the floor on his knees.

The referee couldn't help but show his surprise. He was

slow to order Paul to a neutral corner and slow to begin his count.

"One! Two! Three! Four!"

Fritz staggered up. He fell backwards onto the ropes, which propelled him forward and upright. The fight continued.

Paul moved around the ring and round and round his opponent. Fritz was a bit groggy and tiring fast. Paul wondered how much Fritz's age was affecting him.

Now the crowd wanted the real action: the finale. They didn't need to wait for the full three rounds. They wanted the Aussie challenger to fix this Yank right up and the sooner the better.

Paul knew that he could win. He only had to avoid getting in close. Clinches are the domain of tired boxers, when arms and legs get tangled up so that nobody can deliver a punch. Clinches were a time waster and only measured when judges were awarding points. He wanted to end this fight in this second round, and with a knockout.

Paul knew that Fritz's reach was longer than his. To get a good arm's-length punch in, it would have to get past his opponent's defences and ideally he would want to land two or more for them to be effective. Left and right hooks, or an uppercut, would all be useful but nothing could compare with a full weight of the body-backed arm's-length direct hit to the jaw.

When Fritz at last moved towards Paul, the voices of the crowd rose. Paul swiftly moved forward, bringing his first big punch with him before Fritz could counter. Fritz reeled back but steadied himself and came forward punching the air in front of him.

Paul dropped down to the left and got home another full straight right to the chin. Fritz slumped but did not fall. Then

Fritz went into a classic defensive pose, covering his face while moving forward.

Paul moved around him, making him follow. Paul could not get a third punch to the chin because of his opponent's defensive pose. Then Paul moved in. Getting in close for the first time, he placed an uppercut on Fritz's chin and between his defending gloves. It was so quick hardly anyone saw it. Fritz dropped his hands momentarily and as he did so Paul placed the third straight right to his chin.

Fritz went down for the third time.

"Kill him! Kill him!" chanted the crowd.

The referee was quicker this time. Lester Hammond knew he must act. He had noted the crowd's reaction. The fight had been a big success, although it looked as if he would have to pay out.

"One! Two! Three! … "

Fritz Holland rolled onto his side and attempted to get onto his knees, then fell forward again and was unable to move.

"Eight! Nine! Ten! Out!"

The crowd was beside itself. Hands were thrust into the ring where Paul stood, with everyone wanting to touch him. Paul looked around and raised his hand and nodded and mouthed a "thank you".

The referee held Paul Stoner's arm in the air as he announced him the winner. In the other hand, he waved the ten-pound note to advertise the fact that people did win money at his tent.

He handed Paul the note and turned and looked at him and said, "If you would like to make a lot of money lad, call by in the morning and talk to me. I need a good man like you. I'm getting tired of has-beens."

Paul thought for a moment, then smiled and answered, "One day, maybe."

He saluted his second who stood smiling in the far corner, waved good-bye to the audience and left the tent.

When Paul stepped out from the fight marquee into the fresh air and the silver moonlight, he heard a woman's voice call to him from the shadows of the big cypress tree twenty yards from the tent.

He stopped and looked into the darkness.

The woman walked towards him. She came close and stood in front of him and looked into his face. She looked like someone from an advertisement in a catalogue or newspaper. Or a model, or someone you saw in the movies. Her face was so alive and intense, made even more so by her bright lipstick and the glow of the coloured carnival lights.

"Hello Paul, it's me, Anna."

Was this really Anna O'Malley, from the pub? Kate's sister?

"I'm amazed at what I just saw you do in there, Paul. I'm confused. I don't know who you are."

She put a hand on his arm.

"No one told me you were a boxer. In fact, no one seems to know much about you at all. I'm not even sure why I'm standing here wanting to find out. Suddenly you seem scary. Tell me you are not scary, Paul. I need to know that much about you."

Paul tried to collect his thoughts. His impulse was to laugh, but he saw that Anna was needing real assurances and he reasoned that if she had witnessed him in the ring–and it was the first boxing match she had seen–she was entitled to feel confused and uncertain.

"Hello Anna. No, I'm not scary. I'm just the same bloke you see having a quiet drink with Jack. I've boxed since I was thirteen, and I enjoy it. There! Does that set your mind at rest?"

He gave her a big friendly smile and took her hand from his arm and held it.

Anna moved to stand beside him, then put her arm through his.

"No, Paul, I want to know more. I think you had better come with me. I'll make you a drink, and then you must tell me everything. Please do that for me."

Paul tried to concentrate on the situation but had difficulty. Images of the recent events in the ring were demanding his attention and Anna's arrival had interrupted his thoughts. Her presence confronted him with new challenges. Her voice, her perfume, her need for his attention became intertwined with the afterglow of the fight.

While unbundling his corralled emotions and thoughts, and the scenes in his head resulting from the fight, perhaps he could answer her questions at the same time. Naively, that's what Paul thought.

"If you'd like to, Anna. Where will we go? I should clean up a bit. Gets sweaty in the ring."

Anna looked at him and gave a faint smile. Then she squeezed his arm reassuringly against the side of her body for just a moment and said, "My friend Edna and her sister have a house in Duke Street, just up off the main street. I'm looking after it this weekend while they visit their mother in Colac. We'll go there."

As Anna retrieved the house key from her bag at the front door of the small weatherboard cottage, Paul again attempted to cross-reference his thoughts and establish a footing in a reality in which he was comfortable, but without success. It didn't bother him that he had not yet fully analysed Fritz Holland's motives for the flapping left elbow movement near the end of the first round.

Was it possible that a similar flapping distraction had happened in the notorious Les Darcy fight which resulted in the foul against Darcy?

Nor did Paul try to understand his compliant attitude to Anna's request for him to come with her. Perhaps the blow to the head at the time of the arm flapping had concussed him slightly.

Paul did have some understanding of the situation, though his theory was unproved. He knew from past experience that success in a fight in the ring released something into his system that changed his perceptions of things ever so slightly. Whatever it was, it elevated and then overrode the day-to-day rational thinking of his normal thought processes.

"Make yourself comfortable, Paul, while I put the kettle on.

If you would like to clean up, the bathroom is through there to the right. There is still hot water in the tank if you want to take a shower. Please yourself. Oh, and the toilet is the door next to it."

Anna dropped her bag on the lounge room table and walked into the kitchen.

"Thanks," said Paul as he wandered off to the bathroom.

Hr took a shower and thought how wonderful hot water and soap could make you feel.

When he came back into the lounge, Anna was sitting on the settee holding a cup of tea. She had switched off the main light and put on the reading lamp next to the fireplace.

Paul looked at her as if for the very first time. She looked fantastic. He noticed her tight-fitting dress. Her shapeliness was accentuated by her dress and his gaze could not avoid the stockinged legs and the heeled shoes. Demure, desirable and dangerous, he thought. Or was that the voice of Rod, his boxing ring second, warning him of danger? He smiled sheepishly.

"Feel good?" she asked.

"Really good," he replied.

"Come and sit beside me, Paul. You don't have to talk. I won't put you through all that stuff I spoke about earlier. I've settled down a bit."

"It's not a mystery, Anna. Boxing seems violent to people who don't understand it. Boxers respect their opponents and appreciate each other's technique. Boxing is not a lot different from football."

Paul added a sugar lump to his cup and sat down beside her.

"I think I was a bit taken aback by how the crowd reacted. They were near hysterical towards the end shouting, 'Kill him!' and stuff like that. For a while there, watching you in those last few moments, I really believed that was what you were going to do."

Anna looked at him, intense and questioning.

Paul managed not to laugh or smile.

"Boxing does attract some rough followers and many of them do see it as fighting. But most boxers see it differently. It's a sport they can do well at. They don't walk around picking fights, whereas some of the people who watch them might."

"When I talk to you as we are talking now, I cannot for the life of me believe that it was you I saw fighting tonight. You seem to be a different person."

Anna moved closer to Paul and took his hand in hers, threading their fingers together.

"Despite everything, or maybe it's because of everything, I want to know you better, Paul."

Anna reached across and turned his head to face her, then kissed him firmly on the lips. He kissed her back and caressed her cheek with his free hand. Paul stopped thinking about the fight.

"Let's relax and just enjoy the evening. I'm going to have a lemon cordial. You must be really thirsty. Would you like one too?"

Paul watched Anna get up from the settee. She was slender, and her body moved so easily.

"Yes, I'd love one thanks," he replied.

"Good, I'll make a jug," Anna called back over her shoulder.

While Anna moved around in the kitchen making the drinks, Paul had a moment to reflect. He made a mental note that Anna might be an analytical person like himself. He sensed that she weighed up every word that was said to her, or that she spoke.

If Paul had been less preoccupied with the night's events, he might also have seen that her every gesture, her every smile, and her facial expressions and her words were all calculated to achieve the outcome Anna desired. Anna's beauty along with her years of working in her parents' hotels– where men of every type showed great interest in her–had expanded her catalogue of mannerisms beyond anything that most young women would ever attain.

With clearer observation, Paul might have seen that there wasn't a situation involving men that Anna could not turn to her advantage. Anna could have whatever she wanted.

It was for only a moment, but not long after Paul downed

his third long glass of lemon cordial he experienced a floating sensation quite unlike any he'd experienced before. He sank back into the softness of the settee, laughing at Anna's joke about the question–"What does a whore want most for Christmas?"–and he was halfway through his fourth glass when Anna stood and took his arm, pulled him from the settee and led him into the bedroom.

When Paul woke in the early hours of the morning and saw Anna naked and beautiful on the bed in the fading light of the full moon, he experienced a sensation of satisfaction not unlike the one he'd had when he won the fight. And it was similar to the feeling he had when he successfully completed other things he did, be they breaking in a horse, dynamiting a cliff face on the roadworks, or playing a game of cricket.

He understood that everything he did had a beginning and an end. Only life itself was ongoing. Everything that happened along the way was simply a single passing experience. He saw no connection between what he did each day and how life unfolded over time. The emotional glue that could connect related experiences to create something bigger, something that could influence the future, had failed to develop in him.

A child who grew up alone–with no one to share intimate moments–had no use for such an emotion.

Paul knew that it was time to move on. He leant over and kissed Anna lightly on the cheek. He collected his clothes and went to the lounge room and dressed. Then, shouldering his bag, he left the house and headed for the butcher's paddock.

Anna stretched and turned when she heard the front door

close. Pulling the blankets over her, she smiled and reminded herself that she must not forget to replace Edna's now empty vodka bottle before she left.

There was one other tiny thing vying for Anna's attention: the time of the month. But Anna chose to ignore that little voice.

When the lad found the boxing tent he couldn't have been more surprised. A large sign announced that boxing classes for teenage boys were held each afternoon during the school holidays. He entered the tent. Classes were in progress and he got in line.

It was a warm spring afternoon in the New South Wales coastal town of Nowra and Paul Stoner was helping his young assistant demonstrate techniques to a group of teenage boys.

Paul let his young friend Jimmy lead the proceedings, just acting as a sparring partner and demonstrating moves and body positions, as Jimmy directed.

Paul rarely intervened in the teaching unless asked, being happy to just be the fall guy or dummy.

After a general introduction to basic moves and stance, Jimmy took each lad and sparred with him individually for a few minutes while Paul stood back and watched. Paul didn't pay much attention to the boys' faces, just the body movements as each was instructed.

He was thinking about something else when he became aware that Jimmy was standing staring at him and not working with the boys.

Pulling himself back to the present, Paul smiled at Jimmy and said, "Sorry Jim, what would you like me to do?"

There was silence. Jim did not reply but kept looking at

his boss. Paul sensed that something was not right and looked at each of the lads standing around Jimmy.

Everything seemed perfectly normal, but then his gaze fell on the lad standing beside Jimmy. Immediately Paul felt the hairs on the back of his neck begin to rise and he stopped breathing.

A feeling akin to fear gripped him momentarily. The boy was a mirror image of himself, albeit younger, probably around fourteen. His face, his eyes and hair colour and curl, and his figure were those of a young Paul; even his faint far-away-look smile.

Jimmy could see that his boss had recognised what he had seen. So had the lad, who continued to stare at Paul. The other boys now noticed the similarity and were trying to understand the situation, one shuffling his feet uncomfortably.

Paul slowly moved towards the boy, not wanting to frighten him yet mesmerised by what he was seeing. Then he spoke.

"Lad, would you please tell me your name?"

Again there was silence, then the boy gave a friendly open smile.

"I'm Paul, sir. Paul O'Malley."

5

YOUNG LOVE

"Sheila is coming over tomorrow. We are going to see some friends of hers, then we're heading on over to a house in Wauchope that she's thinking of buying.

"Colin is bringing over the stock we bought on Thursday so you will need to be here to help him unload. Keep them in the yard until I get back and they've settled down. Make sure they have fresh water but don't feed them any hay. They won't need it.

"Oh, and by the way, Sheila will drop off her daughter Cynthia here so you will have company for the day. There's plenty of food in the cupboard so the two of you won't starve. We should be back late afternoon."

Paul's uncle Rodney was ironing a shirt. As the ladies of the town were known to remark, "... he might not have a woman in the house but he manages to keep himself looking smart."

"How come I haven't met her daughter before?" Paul enquired.

"She lives on a property north of the river with her father and his sister and family. He manages the place. She goes to school in Albury and only comes to stay with her mother in the holidays. I reckon she's about your age, maybe a bit older. She's been around livestock all her life so the two of you will have similar interests. Be nice to her. Sheila says she thinks Cynthia gets a bit lonely on the farm."

Sheila arrived early the next day and tooted the horn as she rounded the machinery sheds and pulled up outside the back door.

Paul followed along as Uncle Rodney went out to greet her, not with his usual passionate kiss and energetic hugging, but with a brief hug and peck on the cheek. Paul instantly saw the reason for his uncle's hesitant welcome. A thin suntanned girl with blonde wavy hair stood beside the car surveying the scene.

"Rodney and Paul, this is Cynthia, Cynthia this is Rod and that is Paul his nephew, who lives here with him."

The girl stood very still. Then she looked first at uncle Rod and then at Paul.

"Hello both of you," said Cynthia. "Great place you've got here."

Then without another word, she headed down towards the creek that ran below the cattle yards.

"She will explore everything and drive you crazy with questions," said Sheila, looking at Paul as she spoke. "But you won't find her boring, I can assure you. She can do anything a man can do on the farm. And don't worry if she doesn't answer your questions immediately. She will be thinking about what you said. And she won't always give the answer you expected.

"I'm told Cynthia is a bit different from most fourteen-year-olds. Probably too bright for her own good sometimes. But you will soon get to know her. Best of luck!"

Rod climbed into the driver's seat. He turned the car around and Sheila got in.

Rod leant out of the window and yelled above the noise of the motor, "Don't forget Colin is coming. We should be back between four and five but don't worry if we are late. Enjoy yourselves and we'll see you later."

The tourer leapt forward, then almost stopped before shooting off in fits and starts and disappearing around the corner.

Silence prevailed for just a moment. Then Paul heard a voice calling from what seemed a long way off.

"Can you help me with this please?"

Cynthia waved to him from the far side of the creek. She was hanging onto a rope which was attached to the crayfish trap, except she probably didn't know what was on the end of it. It was snagged on something.

Even at a distance, Paul could see that she was very wet and looked bedraggled. Her clothes clung to her and her hair looked crazy.

Paul headed down to the creek.

"Are you all right?"

Cynthia nodded.

"It's snagged," she answered in a low voice. "If it is a crayfish trap, we should get it up and check it."

"It's not a problem. The door is closed when we're not using it so there won't be anything in it, although sometimes an eel manages to slip in."

Paul untied the thin rope that he used to pull in the heavy rope hanging from the big gum tree, which they swung out on over the water hole on hot days. This time he wasn't using it to drop into the water but just to get him onto the far bank.

Paul dropped to the grass gently, just a few feet from where Cynthia sat. She watched him intently, checking his every movement while cleverly hiding her interest.

"Shouldn't you keep it out of the water when you're not using it?"

"I do, but we had big rains a week or so back and it looks as if a floating tree branch may have dragged it in. I'll get it out now while you are holding the rope. That will make it easier."

Paul waded into the water with his right hand following the taut rope and his left gently moving leaves and debris away in front of him. He quickly located the submerged tree limb and with great effort succeeded in raising a part of it above the water level so that they could see where the rope went. Then the cage appeared, and with a bit of pulling and pushing Paul freed the contraption from its captor. He called to Cynthia to pull the wire net up to the bank.

The two of them stood looking down at the net. Then Paul dragged it further away from the water, all the time watched by the girl.

"Follow me. There is a tree across the water just around the corner. You won't need to get wet again. Are you comfortable, or should I get you a towel to dry off? I'm supposed to look after you. Your mum would be furious if she came back and found you had died of pneumonia."

Paul's attempt at humour had been ignored and he turned to lead them to the river crossing.

Halfway along the track that led up to the house, Cynthia yelled "Chickens!" and ran off towards the fowl pens nestled beneath the two giant peppercorn trees that gave afternoon shade to the homestead.

Paul stopped and watched her, then followed along. Cynthia had already let herself into the chook pens and he could hear the hens' warning cackles as the stranger moved among the nest boxes and the hanging self-feeder drums containing wheat.

"No eggs," came a voice seemingly addressed to itself.

Paul put his head against the wire door of the dark shed and called out. "I collected a dozen or so before you arrived. But I haven't checked the guinea fowl nests yet. Let's do that."

The wacky-looking girl appeared.

"Show me guinea fowl!"

Paul beckoned Cynthia from the yard.

"We go into the scrub over there."

He nodded towards a patch of casuarina trees and wattles, below which long yellow native grasses crowded the woodland floor.

Paul led the way and Cynthia, her still damp dress now covered in short stalks of straw and spider webs from the chook shed, followed, all the time fighting back her usual desire to run in front to explore for new things.

As they approached the trees, Paul let out a series of cackling noises. Cynthia stopped and stood watching him.

Suddenly a bird that Cynthia had never seen before came out of the woodland in front of him followed by many others. Their feathers were blue-grey and interlaced with white ones. They had little necks and tiny funny heads with bluish white scaly skin behind the eyes that reached to the neck, and bright red wattles hung below their beaks. Among the dozen or more fowls there was one that hung back seemingly not wanting to leave the safety of the trees.

Paul pointed to the hen, directing Cynthia who immediately saw the four little chicks dashing in and out between their mothers legs.

Cynthia was thrilled and expressed herself in wild yelling,

which Paul eventually made out was her calling, "Guinea fowls, guinea fowls, guinea fowls. I love you! Guinea fowls are so funny, so funny."

"Where do they live?" Cynthia shouted above the fowls' loud calling. She came and stood beside Paul for the first time instead of standing at a distance somewhere else, as she had done so far.

"They roost over in the peppercorn trees. They are great at guarding the chooks. They make a lot of noise if a fox or eagle comes around. And they nest all over the place but mainly in here in the long grass. Let's have a look."

The two moved out of the sunlight into the shade of the woodland, looking around them as they went. Cynthia suddenly yelled out "Here's a nest!"

Eight eggs lay in a nest of grass and feathers in a hollow among dead roots where a tree had once stood.

Cynthia gathered up the hem of her dress to make a pouch, into which she placed the eggs.

Paul looked appreciatively at her long legs, newly exposed above her knees. He found Cynthia attractive and he was conscious of feeling a pleasurable agitation when he thought about her.

It confused him just a little.

After delivering the eggs to the bowl on the kitchen side-board, Cynthia dashed off to explore the house. Paul didn't try to follow her, but instead brought some bread to the table and then sliced some lamb and found a jar of pickles. He called her name out in the passageway, realising as he did so that it was the first time he had spoken her name.

"Cynthia! Come and have something to eat."

Cynthia was suddenly at his side, having come through the door that led to the wash house. She moved silently and surprised him.

"Who cooks?" Cynthia asked.

"Uncle Rod does and so do I." Paul replied.

Cynthia picked up a piece of meat and laid it on a slice of bread, then wandered back outside. Paul heard the fly wire door bang. He did the same with bread and lamb but added pickle to the lamb, and then went to join her outside.

The girl had disappeared. Then he heard Cynthia's questioning voice.

"Where's your sow?"

Paul didn't answer immediately but walked in what seemed to be the direction of the voice.

For a moment he thought he had come the wrong way, then saw movement up high and spotted Cynthia at the top of the ladder, which stood between two water tanks. She peered in to one then the other, then back to the first one again.

"We get dead possums in our tanks. Dad is always fishing them out."

Paul walked over to stand and hold the ladder to prevent it from sliding over. Uncle Rod had always said he would tie the top of the ladder to the frame running between the tanks, but he'd never got round to doing it.

"We used to, until we put the strips of wire netting over the top. Now we don't get them."

Paul found himself gazing upward and seeing all the way up Cynthia's dress to her knickers. Her brown legs seemed to go on forever and that was exciting. But the part of her body he was attracted to most, after her face and hair, was her perfect feet and ankles.

Paul thought how different life would be if they lived in the same house. Perhaps if Uncle Rod married Sheila, then Cynthia would come and be with them each school holiday. How wonderful that would be. He must think of ways to encourage Uncle Rod to settle down and marry Sheila.

"Where's your sow?" came the question again.

"We don't keep pigs. We go away sometimes for a week or more, fishing or shooting. You can be away from cattle and sheep and you can leave food for chooks, but pigs need daily attention. You can't leave them alone on the place. They wouldn't survive."

Cynthia came down the ladder rapidly, then stood in front of Paul and just stared at him while she finished off her bread and lamb. Then she turned and headed off again, this time towards the row of wooden sheds.

Paul thought she would most likely start at the first one and work her way along, but she didn't. Cynthia in her usual rapid walking style headed to the corner shed, opened the door, went in and closed it behind her.

Paul wondered if this was her way of saying, "Don't follow me" but he hesitated for only a moment before entering.

Cynthia stood transfixed.

This was Paul's and his uncle's training room. They called it the gym. The setup was very spartan, comprising two different sized hanging punching bags and a roped-off boxing ring with a canvas floor covering a thick layer of soft hay.

Hanging on one wall were two rows of boxing gloves. Those on the top row were larger and mostly the same size, while on the bottom row, the sizes went from the very small gloves that Paul had worn some years back to those that he now wore.

"I want to fight you!" Cynthia exclaimed.

Paul laughed.

"You mean you would like to put on the boxing gloves?"

"Yes, and you put some on too."

Cynthia reached up and selected a small pair that looked

to be her size and proceeded to pull them on. Then she stared at the long laces hanging from her wrists.

"What do I do now?" she asked, turning to Paul and holding her hands up.

"I'll tie your laces so that the gloves don't come off when you are boxing," he answered.

"But I can't tie yours while I'm wearing these. So what will you do?"

"Don't worry. I can tie my own. I have a knack using my teeth. Usually there is someone around to do it for you when you are at a boxing match."

Cynthia held her hands up in front of her and watched silently while Paul pulled the laces tight and wrapped and tied them around her wrists. Then he pulled his own gloves on and did a quick thing with his mouth to fix his laces around his wrists and out of the way.

"Are you ready to box, Cynthia?"

Cynthia eyed him with the now familiar stare of a person trying to get the measure of him.

"Yes, Paul."

He liked the way she spoke his name. But then he liked everything she said or did.

Paul took her upper arm in his gloved hand and led her to the ropes of the workout ring. He ducked under the top rope into the ring and Cynthia followed.

Paul moved them to the middle of the ring and showed her how to face him and hold her arms in a defensive stance. Then he backed away and stood in a similar position.

"So Cynthia, if you want to begin by hitting me, that would be a good start. Aim to hit my face and be ready to push my arm away when I try to hit you. Have you got that?"

Cynthia stared at Paul.

"Why would I want to hit you in the face, Paul?"

Paul fought back a smile and answered.

"Well, a boxer aims to beat his opponent by hitting him. They both keep doing this until one gives in or gets knocked unconscious.

"We are not going to do anything like that but you need to know that that is what boxing is about. The winner is the one who fights the best. You get that? Right now we are just sparring, or playing at hitting if you like."

Paul moved his hands about to suggest sparring and Cynthia began waving her hands in a movement that seemed more like swimming.

"Oh yes! The other thing that boxers need to do is to keep their feet and legs moving as if they are dancing. This means that they are all the time changing their position and making it more difficult for the other person to land a direct hit on their chin or nose. Clear on that?"

Cynthia stopped pawing the air and stood and stared at him in her usual disarming way. Then she started to dance, swinging her legs backwards and forwards and side to side, added the swimming movement and so became a bizarre and amazing spectacle to behold.

Paul was mesmerised and slid totally under Cynthia's spell.

If this had been a proper fight, she would have landed half a dozen significant blows to his head, which he might not have survived. As it turned out, he was unprepared for what happened next.

Cynthia suddenly launched herself towards him, and fell and crashed into his chest. Paul managed to catch her in his arms but not before he lost his balance. Together they fell to the floor, he on his back and she lying on top of him.

Cynthia by this time had a gloved hand pressed against each of his ears, and their noses were all but touching. If that wasn't surprising enough for Paul, Cynthia pushed her face close to his and pressed her lips to his lips and they kissed.

The two lay there not moving. The kissing continued and Paul felt passion like nothing he had felt before.

He shook the gloves from his hands and ran them up her back to her shoulders and then down again and over her small buttocks. Cynthia pressed his lips even harder with hers, moving her mouth slowly as though savouring something delicious. Then Paul ran his hands back up her thin frame and out over her shoulders to her bare arms and pulled her tighter to him.

Cynthia shuddered ever so slightly and Paul's body stiffened in response.

This magic moment for the two ended just seconds later. The huge roaring of a truck horn filled their space and a giant motor sounded as though it was about to come through the gym wall.

"Colin!" shouted Paul.

Cynthia rolled off and sat up looking confused.

"It's the truck bringing the stock Uncle Rod bought at the market yesterday. I have to show him where to go."

Cynthia stared at him, trying to take it all in. For the first time she appeared confused and Paul felt a momentary twinge of guilt. But it wasn't really his fault.

He took off and met the truck outside, where it sat with the motor running and Colin waiting for someone to appear.

"This way Colin!"

He headed down past the sheds and round the corner and turned and pointed towards the second loading race.

By the time Colin had turned the truck around and backed up to the race, Cynthia had joined Paul. She stood beside him with her arms bent and her still gloved hands reaching forward.

Colin switched off the motor and jumped down to join the two, staring at Cynthia all the while.

"Gee Paul. I didn't know you had a girlfriend," Colin said with a broad smile.

Paul went red in the face and attempted to introduce Cynthia, but before he had finished saying her name Cynthia replied on her own account.

"I'm Cynthia and I will marry Paul and I will have four babies. That is if I don't die of pneumonia beforehand."

If Paul's day with Cynthia had triggered an emotion akin to love, his second encounter with a girl–or rather, girls–took him somewhere else entirely, somewhere he would never have imagined.

Paul had moved to the city, where he boarded with his Aunt May and where he was apprenticed at the local brewery.

Leaving work one Friday afternoon, he was greeted by the sound of two voices speaking in unison.

"Hello Paul!" they called.

Paul looked across the street and saw the twins from the accounts department, Lola and Rosa.

"Hello!" he called back.

"We want to talk to you, Paul. We are going your way. Come and walk with us."

Paul hesitated a moment, then crossed over to the corner where the girls stood. He smiled at the two as he approached. Their obvious face make-up and smart fashionable clothes made a strong impression on him and he felt he was entering a place he'd never been before.

Up close, he became aware also of the girls' heady perfume. It reached out and enveloped him so that he felt enclosed in their world, a pleasant and exciting world that he knew he wanted to explore.

"We've been wanting to talk to you ever since we saw you win the apprentices boxing match last week. We had no idea that you were a boxer," said the first girl.

"A 'dark horse' is what someone called you," said the second girl.

"Stop. Please!" said Paul. "First you must tell me which of you is Lola and which is Rosa. I'm so confused."

The girls laughed.

"Silly boy. Does it really matter?" said the first one.

"Well, yes it does. You are two people, not one person," Paul replied.

The second girl spoke. "All right, it's easy really. Once you get to know us you will notice many differences. But to help you out until then, just remember a couple of things."

Paul stood still to look at the two and listened.

"I'm Lola and I have a small mole on my chin," she said, placing a finger on her face to show him the spot.

"The other differences are that I usually speak first, though not always. Also, I'm left-handed and Rosa is right-handed. Another thing is that we always share things. Everything!"

"Everything!" repeated Rosa.

"So there you have it Paul," said Lola.

"Simple isn't it?" said Rosa.

Everyone laughed. Lola took Paul's left arm in her right arm and Rosa took his right arm in her left arm and turned him and then all three wandered gently in the direction of Aunt May's house.

As the trio meandered through the streets of tiny workers' cottages in the late afternoon summer sun, the sisters proposed to Paul that the three of them should meet at the boat shed at Studley Park at midday on the following day for a picnic. They said that they knew a quiet spot among the bushes on the other side of the river close to a good swimming hole. "Don't worry about food. We will bring enough. Just your swimming costume and a towel."

Over the years that followed, Paul would remember the exact moment on returning from work on a Monday afternoon, when Aunt May suddenly began to treat him differently: when his aunt first spoke to him not as a lad, but as she would to any adult male like his uncle or the woodman. A different Aunt May now greeted him in the morning and on his return from work in the afternoon.

It was hard to say exactly what was different, but if Paul had been able to analyse the situation he would have noticed that Aunt May no longer made jokes or acted in a motherly fashion. No longer was Paul the recipient of pudding bowls when May made a chocolate cake. All he knew was that the change in her attitude was abrupt and he could never work out why. It wasn't a problem in any way. Just a little odd; a mystery.

Deep down, Paul could not help linking this moment of change in his aunt with something momentous that had happened to him at the picnic with Lola and Rosa two days before.

But how could that be?

He had had one last swim in the Yarra River before arriving home well washed, his skin positively shining. And before he left his aunt's house, he had told her simply that he was meeting friends and going for a swim.

What had he missed?

. . .

Monday was washing day at May's house, as it was in every home across the country.

As May sorted the dirty linen into separate piles, she couldn't help noticing the sudden waft of an unexpected scent when she picked up Paul's towel. A woman's perfume?

May paused, then laid the towel aside. She knew what she wanted to look for next. She found and dragged Paul's underpants from the pile of dirty washing and carried them out the laundry door away from the smells of the rest of the washing.

Outside, Aunt May sniffed and yes, there was the same perfume smell. But this could have come from the undies being close to the wet towel for the past day or more. And who knows who might have borrowed and shared Paul's towel?

Then May looked closely at the underpants and discovered three faint red patches near the fly buttons. May held the pants close to her face and sniffed again.

"Lipstick!" she declared out loud.

In May's mind, Paul had come of age and she knew that from now on, his world would be very different.

6

ANIMAL INSTINCT

Sos Semple had been working in the little coastal town for six weeks before anyone knew he was there. This was unusual. Kevin at the Co-op knew about the new man working on the dredge, but not until Sos had been there for a few weeks.

Kevin mentioned the newcomer to Jake one day. It was a quiet moment around mid-morning and the big concrete and corrugated iron Co-op building was empty but for the two of them.

"Have you met the new fella on the dredge, Jake?" Kevin asked casually as he wrote out the docket. He bent low over the counter the better to see what he was writing.

"No, I didn't know the job had been filled," replied Jake.

Both men were quiet for a moment, then Jake said, "I reckon I'd go mad pumping sand over that sea wall and watching it wash back in again on the next big tide."

"Someone has to do it," said Kevin, straightening up and looking at Jake.

Jake took the docket from Kevin's outstretched hand and checked that he'd got all he came in for, then got out his chequebook and wrote a cheque for the purchase.

"I take it you've met him, Kevin. What's his name?"

"Mervyn came in with him yesterday to help load the heavy mesh they get for the rock wall repairs. Introduced him as Sos. Can't figure that name. Anyway, there's something about the bloke. Can't figure him either.

"You can usually get a feel of what someone is like when you first meet them, but this fella … ? And when I asked him how long he'd been on the *Sand Groper*, Mervyn jumped in ahead of him and said he'd been here six weeks, but that he was living out at Colac until he found accommodation for himself and his wife in the town and that what with the travelling and early starts and late finishes on the dredge at this time of the year, he–that is Sos–hadn't really been on shore during shop hours."

Kevin stopped talking and stood quietly for a moment.

"All the years I've known Mervyn, I've not heard him say more words than he did then. And he spoke real fast too, like he'd read it somewhere, then rehearsed it. Anyway, I suppose we weren't meant to know everything or life would be too darned dull, wouldn't it?"

He grinned and pulled himself up straight, becoming the jovial Kevin everyone was used to seeing behind the counter.

Jake laughed. Kevin was good value. Even the grumpiest and gloomiest old bachelor farmers saw the good in Kevin and respected him for it.

Jake loaded his trailer. He'd bought a pack of first grade pine to make this season's new bee boxes. He was getting started earlier this year. Last year the honey flow came early and he'd lost too many bees through the premature build-up of numbers in the hives and the swarming that followed.

. . .

It was a month after his conversation with Kevin that Jake met Sos Semple.

Alan Wilminck, Jake's nearest neighbour was about to begin shearing his sheep and it was usual for farmers on adjoining properties to help out with each other's seasonal farm chores. Jake was there at seven o'clock sharp to get Alan's instructions.

The shearing shed and yards nestled at the end of a small valley. They had a northerly aspect, ideal for drying and warming sheep before and after shearing.

Steep hills rose around the valley and Jake could see there was a flock far up on the hill and he knew there was another bigger flock in the scrubby valley on the other side where it bordered his own property. Alan had brought a third mob in late yesterday afternoon so as to be certain that there were dry sheep available for the shearers when they arrived that morning.

The shearers were already geared up and ready to drag in their first sheep when Jake arrived. Other farmers drifted in or about, greeting each other with calls or friendly taunts.

"Wouldn't she let you get out of bed?" called one man to young Stephen, who had got home from his honeymoon less than a month earlier. Then the sound of the shearing machines made talking more difficult, and Alan beckoned to Jake to come outside.

"Same as last time?" said Jake.

"Reckon so Jake, if that's all right with you? If you bring down the mob on the north slope first and put them in the river paddock, that should give us about the right number to shed tonight.

"If the boys get through what's in there early, then they can bring some of the new mob through to the yards without losing them with the lot going out. Then you can bring down the rest and put them in the house paddock.

"Look out for the kids' new pony when you get to the home gate. She doesn't much like sheep and she's just as likely to push them back through the gate at you. Send one of the dogs ahead after her if she's hanging about the gate, that'll give you time to get them through."

Alan paused to think if there was anything else to tell Jake before he went back inside.

"Oh, I nearly forgot, Jake. There's a bloke coming out for a look. He's the new fella on the dredge. He should be out around smoko. His name is Sos. Doesn't know anybody so I thought he might get to meet people out here and have a look around.

"Thought he could work with you on moving stock around. Use him on gates and yelling at the right time.

"You're good with people Jake, you'll work out what to do with him."

Alan took off his hat and pushed his white hair back off his forehead before resting the cap back on top of it. He grinned his wonderful broad grin, called the farm dogs and told them to go with Jake, then went back into the shed.

Jake checked the gates around the immediate area before heading up the hill with Sally and her eighteen-month-old pup Cocoa, along with Alan's two border collies.

The three-kilometre climb to the top of the hill, collecting the mob and making sure he had them all, then bringing them back down would take around two hours. Jake reckoned he should be back for smoko.

Jake was now doing what he loved most–walking the hills of the Otways, the range of hills that followed the coast-line and looked out over the Southern Ocean. He spent most of his time alone, usually outside working with stock on his farm or moving his beehives around the honey flows of the region.

When Jake and the dogs were ready to bring the sheep down, he stopped to look out at the beautiful scenery beyond and far below.

The house and sheds were like toys and the first newly shorn sheep were tiny bright white dots. A car moved silently along the river road, turned into the driveway and parked under the trees next to the other cars. A figure got out and stood still for a few moments before disappearing into the shed.

Jake stood up and called Sally to heel, then sent Cocoa and the other dogs out to the far left of the sheep spread out below them. Then he called out "Yo, yo, yo," loudly, waving his arms at the same time to start the animals moving and telling Sally to "speak out". Sally moved out to the right where she could view the proceedings, barking loudly as she moved.

The flock began to bunch up into a mob and move down the slope. Jake recalled the three dogs and they walked quietly down the hill behind the sheep. Half an hour later they came close to the house paddock gate in the fence that ran alongside the river paddock.

Alan was there with the bloke from the dredge.

Alan had chased the pony away and had opened the gate, then gone to stand outside the small paddock and up along another track so that the sheep would not head off that way.

In moments the sheep were through to the river paddock and the gate secured. Then the three men began walking down to the shed together.

"Jake, this is Sos, who I told you about," said Alan.

"Pleased to meet you," said Jake turning and thrusting out his hand. Sos shook the hand less than enthusiastically. "Hello," he muttered back. "Didn't know yer had hippies working for yer, Alan." A smile that could easily have been a sneer crossed his face.

"Doesn't work for me, Sos," replied Alan with a good-natured laugh. "Jake farms the property next door and is also an apiarist. He's smart enough to farm bees and trees as well as sheep and cows. He's a wizard with livestock and a great neighbour. Always around if I need help with anything."

Alan, thinking the horse was chasing the young dog, called Cocoa away from the pony who was following too closely.

Sos kept looking around at the pony nervously. When he stopped and turned to face the horse, it reached out towards him with its ears laid back, its nostrils flared and its lips curled upwards and showing its teeth. Then it turned its back towards him and kicked the air with its back legs.

Sos ducked and swore under his breath and Jake slapped the horse hard on its rump and yelled at it to "get away, off".

Alan stood staring at the pony. "I've never seen it behave like that before. I'd better mention it to the kids."

Sos seemed to make a point of keeping away from Jake during smoko, and when the gong sounded he moved out to the yards to work the race gate, letting the sheep through twenty at a time for penning up near the catcher and the shearers.

Sos had got talking to Stephen during the break. Stephen was in charge of sheep movements from the holding paddocks through to the shearing stands.

Jake stayed at the sheds for a short time to get the feel of how things were running. The shearers were brothers and in top form, working at a pace which they knew they could keep up for the full day.

Outside, Stephen was to show Sos how to operate the sorting gate and regulate the number of sheep moving towards the ramp and up into the shed.

Sos indicated straight away that he knew what to do and Stephen called his dogs and moved out into the big yard to send sheep down the curved funnel race to where Sos would fill two races at a time, each with twenty sheep.

Stephen moved his dogs gently into the mob and sent the first group of sheep into the funnel race.

Jake watched and admired Stephen's gentle stock-handling methods, both with his dogs and the sheep. Then he noticed that things were not working out quite the way he'd expected.

As the sheep moved quickly along the curved narrowing walkway to within three metres of the race gate and Sos, the front sheep halted, stiffened their front legs and leaned back-wards, and no matter how much pressure Stephen and his dogs applied at the rear, the lead animals refused to move forward.

It was quite normal in this situation for sheep to hesitate when they first spotted the gate operator, but then they would always move forward, sometimes with a great bound through the gate past the operator and run on, believing that the race would provide a means of escape.

This wasn't happening.

Stephen told Sos to stand very still and not look directly into the eyes of the sheep. Sos went rigid and turned his head, seemingly looking elsewhere. Stephen and the dogs resumed their urging but the sheep did not move forward.

Stephen then called to Sos to squat down behind the

waist-high sheet-iron fence panel. Again, Stephen and the dogs urged the sheep to move on, but the sheep did not move.

Leaving the dogs to hold the sheep from moving backwards, Stephen went up to where the front sheep stood. He quickly climbed the race fence, and taking the animal firmly in a headlock, he dragged it through the race gate and up towards the ramp. He gently let it go and hopped out of the race, quietly telling Sos to stay put. With one sheep now through the gate, well up the race and in full view of the other sheep that would surely want to follow, Stephen called for the dogs to "speak up" and push the mob forward. But again, the sheep refused to move. Stephen repeated the earlier process so that there were now two sheep up at the far end of the ramp. This time he joined the dogs towards the back of the mob, yelling and physically pushing the animals, but still they would not move forward.

Stephen stopped for a moment. Jake watched him take his dogs and walk back and around in a circle thinking about what he would do next. Jake knew a lot about animal behaviour and he respected Stephen's judgement and handling abilities. He thought about what he would do in Stephen's position and knew he would have done exactly the same.

Animals can surprise, but not usually at times like this. Fear and confinement would cause the sheep to act in a predictable way and follow what they saw as an escape route. Occasionally, one sheep would prop, but it was apparent that all the sheep here were acting in the same way. Jake ran through his catalogue of experience with sheep and other livestock and came to one simple conclusion – fear – but fear of what?

Stephen stopped walking back and forth and stood looking at the gate through which the sheep would not pass.

Jake knew that he had come to the same conclusion as himself.

Stephen walked up to where Sos was still squatting behind the fence and said something to him. Sos stood up and climbed out of the enclosure.

Stephen pointed down to where the dogs were resting a few metres behind the sheep, giving a half-circle motion with his hand.

Sos walked away from the sheep towards the yard fence, then turned and followed it down until he came level with the dogs and moved in behind them.

Stephen gestured that it was the right spot and that he was not to move until instructed. Even as he climbed over the low fence to take Sos's place on the gate, the sheep were filing through, rapidly filling the first race. Within moments, he had swung the gate behind twenty animals and was busy filling the next race.

Jake got up, called to Sally and Cocoa, and began his climb up the hill to bring down the last flock. As he moved comfortably along the narrow contour tracks formed by farm animals over many years, he thought about Sos Semple and what he had just seen. He wondered what sort of man Sos really was.

Over the next few months the name Sos Semple became well known in the district.

He and his wife Janice bought the most admired small farm in the area just minutes from the town centre. It had been on the market for a considerable time at a price no one thought anybody could ever afford. It included a brick house with a beautiful garden and ocean views. It had been built by a Catholic order as a residence and farm for priests. The paddocks were well fenced and the shedding superb.

A herd of top-quality Angus cows with calves at foot and

accompanied by a pedigreed bull appeared on the property as though they had fallen from the sky. No one saw the stock truck arrive in town or the animals being unloaded. And suddenly there was a new truck complete with a new stock crate, and a freshly painted sign on the shiny green doors read "Semple's Angus Stud Apollo Bay" along with the telephone number.

The town was abuzz with talk about the Semples. Everything from "What did this bloke know about breeding stud cattle?" to "How could someone who was working on the dredge one minute own a million dollars worth of farm and stud stock the next?"

All this and more filtered through to Jake from conversations he overheard while waiting to be served at the bakery or filling the ute at the Ampol garage on his twice-weekly trip into town.

At the Co-op, Kevin seemed to have decided not to be involved in any discussions about Sos Semple. Whenever two or three men met at the Co-op remarks about Sos Semple would soon crop up such as, "How's he going to make his money on that place at the prices stock are fetching these days?" and "Where would he have got the money for all that?"

"None of my business," Kevin would answer if someone tried to draw him into the conversation. And he would remain intent on writing up his dockets or go out to the back of the store in search of a certain sized bolt or hose fitting, always either not hearing the conversation or removing himself from the men altogether.

On one of those quiet days when Jake came into the Co-op and the two were alone, Kevin did speak about Sos Semple, though he did not use the man's name.

"Mervyn said he's thankful that bloke's gone from the

dredge," Kevin said quietly while looking up the price of a roll of roofing felt in his big book.

There was silence for a moment while he wrote it on the docket, then he continued.

"Mervyn told me in strict confidence, Jake, that he was told he had to employ him on orders from high up in the Marine Board in Melbourne. It was all hush-hush and the man had to be protected from anyone who might come looking for him or asking questions. Anyway, Mervyn said the bugger didn't lift a finger the whole time he was on the dredge and that having him there was the most unpleasant experience of his whole life."

Kevin handed Jake the docket and stood looking at him. "Something is not right, Jake, and I worry about it. I know I shouldn't. But I reckon it's weird how that place was built by priests and now, well I reckon the devil's living there." Kevin went quiet. He wanted Jake to say something.

Jake wrote his cheque and when he finished he looked back at Kevin and smiled, then said, "All I know, Kevin, is that if any man has done something he shouldn't have, he might run, but in the end he can't hide. If there's something wrong here then it will come to its proper conclusion. For the moment, I'd love to see you less worried about it all."

Kevin let out a sigh and replied, "You're right Jake. I'll give up thinking about him for a while."

They both laughed.

Jake was just taking off his bee veil and white overalls when he heard Dusty Rhodes's station wagon coming up the track to the house.

Jake had been away three days working his bees and, in that time, everything on the farm seemed to have run amuck.

It was the weather. An early change had brought sunshine and warmth on top of the heavy rains of the previous week. The pasture seemed to have grown six inches and fruit trees in the orchard were suddenly in bloom.

Some of the hives in the home paddock were already building up to swarm, and cows that Jake thought were not due for a fortnight or more, had dropped big healthy calves in unexpected parts of the farm. He was flat out catching up with all that had happened.

"Hello Jake," Dusty called out through the car window as he turned towards the cattle yards.

Jake had called the vet early that morning to check a heifer that had been in labour for quite some time and seemed to be in trouble.

"Hi Dusty. Bet you're busy this week. I've got her in the shed."

When Dusty had finished his inspection and given the beast an injection, he said he'd call back in the morning as he would be going past, unless Jake rang to say she had calved. The calf felt very big and it was possible he'd have to perform a caesarian.

"Got time for a cup of tea or coffee?" said Jake. "Water's hot. It can be quick."

"Why not?" said Dusty. "I'll just organise my gear in the car and meet you up in the house. Tea please."

Over tea and buttered Boston bun the two spoke briefly about the weather and current farming news.

"I read about your opposition to live sheep sales to the Middle East, Dusty," said Jake. "Nice to see someone sticking their neck out, especially when they're prepared to risk their livelihood. I hope you didn't get up the noses of too many of your bigger customers."

Jake poured more hot water into the teapot.

"It hasn't been too bad," Dusty replied.

Jake sensed that Dusty didn't really want to talk about it. It was something someone did, and that was that.

"Jake, I wanted to ask you about the new owners at the old Church Farm down in the town. Do you know them?" Dusty sounded deliberately casual, as though the question was not of great importance.

"The Semples, I think you mean? Yes, I've met Sos Semple. Alan next door invited him around during shearing a couple of months back. I haven't seen him since then." Jake buttered some more bun.

"I called there this morning to look at their bull," Dusty replied.

"It's a fine-looking bull. I've admired it from the road," said Jake.

"It's not any more. I put it down a couple of hours ago."

Jake looked up from his bun buttering.

"What on earth happened? It must be the safest farm around. Did another bull get in or was it sick? What was wrong with it, Dusty?"

Dusty sipped his tea thoughtfully.

"The beast was very badly injured around the head and neck."

He fell quiet again.

"I've seen many animal injuries over my thirty or so years as a vet, but I've never seen any like this. It was lying down in the cattle crush where it must have collapsed. Its head was a terrible mess which I won't describe but there were no marks, not even mud or blood anywhere on the body beyond the head and neck."

"What did Sos Semple say had happened?" asked Jake.

"He wasn't there. His wife phoned early this morning and

she was there when I arrived. She said her husband was away working.

"Mrs Semple said her husband told her he had found the bull staggering around near the yards when he got up this morning and that he had managed to get it into the crush so that it could be treated. Then he'd had to leave to pick up stock somewhere away from town.

"Mrs Semple also said how her husband had told her the week before that the bull was very aggressive and to watch out for it and that it might just get itself into trouble one day."

Dusty took another sip of tea and stared into the open stove firebox.

Jake knew that Dusty wasn't in the habit of talking about his clients. The fact that he was doing so now meant that he was genuinely concerned. He wasn't just making conversation.

Jake didn't feel that he could question Dusty but, nevertheless, felt a need to understand what had gone on.

"Did Mrs Semple give any clues to what might have happened?" he asked.

"No, she didn't." Dusty paused to reach for another piece of bun.

"The neck-hold on the crush was open. This meant that the animal was better able to lie down or fall down. When I made the comment that the animal could have escaped easily and that I wondered why her husband hadn't locked the crush neck-hold before he left for work to ensure that I could attend to it on arrival, she answered that he had but she had opened the neck-hold when she found the animal sagging and wanting to lie down."

"Well," said Jake, "isn't that what we would do under those circumstances?"

Dusty looked at Jake as though he was searching his face for clues.

"Have you seen the size of this woman? I reckon Mrs Semple would have trouble lifting a half-full shopping basket. Not only could she not reach the overhead release handle, even if she climbed up and swung on it, she would not be able to release the lower safety catch at the same time. And even if she could reach it, I doubt she would have the weight to move the handle. It's a very big crush.

"No, there is something not right in all of this but I'm dammed if I can put my finger on it."

Dusty sighed noticeably and got up from the table. "Thanks Jake, if I don't hear from you I'll call again in the morning."

"Thanks Dusty."

Jake gathered his wire-strainer and tin of staples and a hammer and pliers and gloves and headed off up the hill to fix a small hole in the fence that divided his place from Alan's.

When Jake got back from fencing, he checked the heifer in the barn. To his surprise and joy, she was happily suckling a sturdy calf. Well, that's today's good news, he thought.

Jake began loading the panel van with bee gear.

Tomorrow he would start his rounds of the hives he had in six bush locations close to home. All were likely to need an extra box to cope with this early honey flow. If there was not room in the hives for the bees to store the new honey, then he could lose bees that swarmed and went in search of new homes.

Prevention was everything at this time of the year.

As he worked through the day, snippets of information

about Sos Semple would pass before him, each trying to fit itself with another piece.

The odd behaviour of the sheep when Sos was on the sorting gate at Alan's shearing shed, even the horse's reaction to him. And now the mystery of what happened to Sos's bull. And the very large amounts of money spent on the farm and on setting up the stud.

Jake left early next morning for the hives. He worked on these late into the day until all were fitted with new boxes and secured.

Jake went into town the following morning to buy food and more supplies from the Co-op.

"Have you heard the news, Jake?"

"What news, Kevin?"

"Sos Semple," said Kevin.

"What about Sos Semple?" replied Jake.

"He's dead."

"What?" Jake said.

"Yesterday, multiple bee stings they reckon. His truck must have overheated. The bonnet was up. The mail-truck driver found him on the Wild Dog Creek road. Said she couldn't recognise his face 'cause it was so badly swollen. He was still holding the empty jerry can and was about half a mile from the truck and heading back towards the Huggens's farm. I thought you would have heard about it, Jake."

Jake stared at Kevin with a look of disbelief, then recovering slightly said, "No, I worked over near Lavers Hill all yesterday. Didn't get back till late. You're the first person I've seen to speak to. Do you know if he was alone when it happened?"

"As far as I know, he was."

"You know more about bees than anyone else around here, Jake. Does the story make sense to you? Could bees do that so quickly that he just couldn't escape?"

Jake looked at Kevin for a few moments then spoke, picking his words carefully.

"Yes, Kevin, they could have. Sos may have spotted a swarm hanging off a branch of a tree or a nest of bees in a hole and thrown a rock or stick at it and stirred the bees up.

"Something must have upset them. People work with bee swarms all the time without getting stung.

"And bees die shortly after they sting someone or something, so they really do have to be convinced about the danger to their nest or hive, and their queen, before they commit mass suicide. There is no point in dying for no reason," said Jake.

"Is that a fact?" replied Kevin softly, staring intently at Jake.

"So what if Sos Semple didn't mess about with the bees, Jake, what do you think could have happened?" asked Kevin cautiously.

Jake looked at Kevin, then in a very quiet voice he said, "Only the bees would know that, Kevin, and they, like Sos Semple, are dead."

The two men stood in silence for a moment. Then Kevin muttered "Amen" and disappeared through to the back of the store.

7

SPIN

"Look Jamie, look! Baby lambs everywhere!"

Jamie glanced up from his device long enough to look out of the car window. The landscape was bright green even though the country was in a severe drought. Then he saw the tell-tale black mini water-wheels, signalling that they were passing through an irrigation area. Still pumping scarce water to fatten lambs. Jesus! Will we never get it right? he asked himself.

"Very nice, lovely little lambs, Gran."

"And if they're very lucky, they will become missionaries when they grow up."

It was a few moments before what Gran had said registered with Jamie. He was quite busy typing a reply to a question on a forum which wanted information about alternative coding for a new smart-phone application.

"Missionaries? What do you mean, Gran?"

"I heard all about it on the radio, dear. Australia must keep sending live sheep and cattle overseas, to places where the people haven't yet learned to be kind to animals.

"Australia already has people in those places teaching

meat workers how to kill animals nicely, in the same way we do here. These lambs we can see here might be chosen to go there and help. We need to send lots of them because those people need a lot of animals to practise their humane killing methods. It's true. It was on the radio, dear."

Jamie stopped typing and looked at his grandmother intently. No, this was not one of her little tricks to stop him using his smart phone; she was for real.

"Apparently, these people didn't have a God like ours who taught us to be kind to all living things. So we Aussies, with the help of thousands of sheep and cattle, are going there to put things right."

Jamie wanted to laugh, but his mind was too busy sorting through what Gran had just said. Did she really believe this?

Jamie knew all about spin and fake news. What thinking nineteen-year-old didn't? He and his friends saw it all the time on social media and stuff, but this seemed truly bizarre. Did other people think like she did, he wondered; or was his grandmother a one-off?

Jamie was enjoying his week-long stay at his grandparents' country property.

Grandpa was much slower in his movements than his grandson remembered him from his previous visit. He was only thirteen then, and he remembered touring the outback property with his grandfather in the ute. That was nearly six years ago and since then Grandpa had turned eighty; plus he'd had an accident with the tractor which, while not life-threatening, had left him with recurring pain in his left leg if he walked too far, or when he drove for too long.

This time Jamie drove the ute.

The vast Western District pastoral property carried around fourteen thousand sheep and a couple of hundred cattle.

These days a farm manager–who also owned and managed his own farm close by–looked after the physical day-to-day working of the property, with Grandpa often going out with him to help sort stock. Grandpa was happy to open paddock gates or operate a race gate to sort stock and let his manager worry about mustering, and checking dams and fixing fences.

"We're still de-stocking because of the drought, Jamie. Can't see an end to it myself. People says it's nothing to do with climate change but I think they might be wrong. I haven't seen seasons like this in my lifetime. Wool's down, so feeding animals is not profitable. We'll keep a couple of thousand breeders I expect. The rest can go to the Middle East.

Now lad, head over towards those casuarinas. There's a dam there I keep meaning to look at."

Jamie swung the wheel and took the track towards a line of trees quite a distance off on the horizon.

Off to one side sheep were spread out for what seemed like kilometres, in a slow-moving wave of orange animals on orange dust. Then, in a voice that sounded as though he was talking only to himself, Grandpa said, "One could drive from here across to the Indian Ocean and not see a sheep lying down.

"Millions of sheep are walking all day and into the night poking about in the dust, looking for a feed; roots mainly, but even old weathered sheep shit, the bark off trees, anything they can put into their stomachs. They don't have the time to lie down … unless it's to die."

Jamie knew about the drought. The environment was the major topic of interest amongst his wide range of university friends, both at home and abroad. Their knowledge was extensive and in their scientific fields of study, whatever their subjects–chemistry, biology, botany, statistics, engineering, physics, geology, medicine, even astronomy, and more–they could all find useful ecological and environmental niches to shine a light on.

But being here in the middle of it was different. Just seeing sheep not able to stand still or lie down, and knowing it was like this across much of the continent, gave Jamie a feeling he didn't often allow himself, anger. Anger at the stupidity of people who you wanted to believe would know better than to let the planet get this fucked-up.

"Grandpa, how do sheep get sent away for the live export market? It must be only when a boat arrives at Portland? Portland is the loading place for stock from around here, isn't it?"

"That's right Jamie. A fortnight before a ship arrives in Portland, the exporter or their agent calls growers who have registered with them as having livestock to go, and gives them a date when they will be accepting stock into the loading yards. We then confirm that we will be sending stock and give them an estimate of the numbers. It works out well most times apparently, unless there is a problem with wet weather, and that doesn't happen much."

"Are you registered for the next boat, Gramps?" asked Jamie.

"No, but we are for the third one, after we've shorn the last of the wethers. That will be about mid-June, in eight weeks roughly, and we figure that by then we'll have around two thousand head to go."

The ute slowed as Jamie guided it towards a long dam bank in front of the row of trees. He drove slowly around one end of the bank so that they could look into the dam. He wasn't prepared for what he saw.

A tiny pool of water filled the bottom of the huge bare

concave, surrounded by a five-metre rim of mud. A large female kangaroo was stuck in the mud. Jamie knew that the animal was still alive. The upper part of her body was still upright and even though her eyes were closed, he knew she would be leaning over if she were dead. A metre away was the body of her joey, face down in the mud and obviously dead.

"Oh no. Poor sod. I should have got here earlier," muttered Grandpa. "Well, we can back up and get a rope on her and dig around her and pull her out; or we've got a rifle behind the seat if you want to shoot her. Your call, Jamie."

It took only a moment for Jamie to decide to get the 'roo out. It wasn't that he couldn't shoot her, just that he figured that she probably would survive once she was freed, so that was what he would do.

They backed the ute down as close as they could to where the animal was stuck.

Grandpa went to the back and got out a length of rope and a webbed belt saved from old horse harness and sometimes used to get stranded sheep out of dams. He bent and put the rope loop onto the tow-bar, then passed the rolled up bundle of rope to Jamie to lay out. Then he motioned to Jamie to look in the ute for a half-dozen old boards he carried to lay on the soft mud to walk on.

Jamie took out three boards and turned and walked as far as he could before the mud became too soft. Then he laid down a plank and walked out further and put down another. He had almost reached the kangaroo and when he straightened up and looked at her, he saw that one eye was watching him. Then the other opened and they stared at one another.

Jamie returned to the ute.

"We've got a water bottle, have we Gramps?" he asked.

"Yep, sure have, son." Grandpa reached into the back of the car and passed out an old army flask.

"Thanks," Jamie answered, and picking up the rope he headed out on the planks.

When Jamie came close to the 'roo, he made soft reassuring sounds, saying, "Easy girl; everything will be all right real soon." He adjusted the last plank to get up close; then he placed a hand on the kangaroo's back. She didn't move. He uncorked the water bottle and, with one hand holding one side of her mouth open, he placed the metal neck in between her gums and teeth and poured a little water into her mouth. She still didn't move and he poured a bit more in; then her neck moved involuntarily as it took in the water.

More water and more swallowing followed until Jamie thought she'd had enough. Then he walked halfway back to where his grandfather was waiting and holding a shovel.

"Thanks."

He dug first in front of the animal, being careful not to go down too far to where her long feet must be buried, then at the back and on each side to where the base of her tail would be.

"Doing a good job, lad," called his grandfather. "Just say if I can help."

Jamie stood upright and smiled back at him.

"Looking good so far. Fingers crossed, Gramps."

Jamie fastened the harness around the waist of the animal, just under her elbows, and joined the rope to it. He wondered whether it was the right place. "We'll try that," he murmured to the 'roo and himself.

"Can you do the driving, Gramps?" Jamie called.

"Sure can. Put your hand up and yell 'Stop!' if you want me to stop. Are you ready now?"

"Ready."

As Jamie stood in the hot sun waiting for Grandpa to make his way slowly up the bank to the ute, he reflected on how one's circumstances could change so dramatically. At one moment he was immersed in study in the university library, looking forward to an evening out with friends at an inner-city bar, hidden in an old bluestone-floored warehouse that many years before had housed hundreds, maybe thousands of wool bales. Then, within what seemed like only hours, he was sharing his physical space with a kangaroo in a place where the hand of man was very evident but where the true master was neither a computer chip designer, a mathematician or a dictator, but the weather, or rather, the natural environment.

Jamie saw that his situation was really not a lot different from that of the furry animal beside him, except he wasn't stuck in the mud. Being out here with his grandparents put him closer to reality than all the books in the library would ever do.

As the ute took up the slack and the rope grew taut, Jamie put his arms around the animal and lifted. He needed to be careful not to end up off the plank and in the mud. Slowly but surely she lifted in slow motion until she was fully out of the mud and partly standing on the same plank as Jamie.

Jamie put his hand in the air and called "Stop!", and stood trying to work out what to do next. He loosened his arms from around the kangaroo slowly, watching to see if she stayed standing up. She wavered for a moment, then pulled herself nearly upright.

Jamie realised that he should have put down two planks side by side, as the animal needed a wider path than he did.

Just as he was deciding whether to go and get another plank, the kangaroo leant forward, placed her front paws on the plank and moved her back legs up towards them so that one leg was on the plank while the other touched the top of the mud only gingerly. She then repeated the move and within moments was out of the wet muddy area and onto the harder dry mud.

Jamie was thrilled. Then the kangaroo stood up and looked around and stared at Jamie as though to say, "Well, are you coming or not?"

Jamie laughed, but realised that things were not over yet. He needed to get the harness off the animal quite quickly before it made up its mind that it was time to leave. He approached her slowly as she stood looking at him. He knew that she was quite weak, but perhaps not so weak that she couldn't become difficult to deal with if she got excited.

To his delight, she stood still as he unclipped the harness and drew it slowly away from around her chest.

"There, does that feel better?" he said softly. "Now how do I know you won't head back into the dam?"

"Well done Jamie. I don't think there is much more you can do unless we go home and get one of the big plastic water bowls and a bit of feed of some kind."

On the way back to the house, Jamie's grandfather said how he'd thought about not having checked that dam for three nights in a row and then each day something came up and he'd forget about it. He said he felt ashamed but also embarrassed that he so often forgot things these days.

The two men loaded a large plastic bin and filled two ten-litre cans of water from the shed tank. Then Grandpa grabbed a bucket and half-filled it with grass pellets. He pointed to the nearby hay shed and told Jamie to get a wafer of hay. Then they headed back towards the dam. Jamie thought this was a good moment to ask about Grandma.

"Does Grandma forget things too, Gramps?" Jamie asked, renewing the recent conversation.

"No, she's good, your grandma. She does drive me mad though, sometimes."

"Why is that, Grandpa?"

"She listens to too much talk-back radio and she's always coming up with crazy ideas because of it. She usen't to be like that. I've got my theories about it but I doubt anyone would listen," he said.

"What's your theory, Gramps? I'll listen," replied Jamie, with a supporting laugh.

"Well, there was a time when radio and even television were important. They gave us the news and entertainment. Important things when you live out in the bush.

"It started about twenty years ago I reckon, nothing seemed important any-more. The world just got too big. No one wanted to take a serious look at things because it either took too long or, if it was presented as serious, people no longer wanted to know.

"People wanted instant everything, or they thought they did. Well I started watching and listening, and over time I worked out what had happened."

"You've got me, Grandpa. What happened?"

"What happened, Jamie, coincided with what was going on in the world. The discovery of amazing new technologies, and the concentration of investment in huge single corporate entities which we put under the label 'globalisation,' were the big things that happened.

"When that happened, along came new influences in mass-communication. Of them, the major two things were 'spin' and 'sound bites'."

Jamie's grandfather stopped for a breath.

Jamie was impressed with his grandfather's perceptive understanding of the modern world. But then why wouldn't he be able to see how things really were? Grandpa was an intelligent man. He had been a university student in the 1950s, earning honours in mathematics and law. He had chosen to become a farmer later in life when he inherited the farm of his grandparents.

"So, what we've got now is a bucket full of babble. And your Gran is a prisoner of it."

Jamie thought this might be an opportunity to mention the live-animal trade, to get his grandfather's views on it.

"What you are saying, Gramps, I understand and agree with. It seems to me that the use and effects of 'spin' instead of natural exposition or reportage in the media, are more serious than people think.

"An example that you might not agree with me on, is the question of our live-animal trade. I would like to see it stop, and I, and many of my friends, actively promote banning it.

"Now you might not agree with me on this, Grandpa, but I mention it because, on the way to the farm on Friday, Grandma told me how she believed the sheep going overseas were like missionaries.

"Along with the Australian meat industry advisers, they would make it possible for people in foreign countries, who hadn't had an understanding God like ours, to teach them how to be kind to animals.

"I must say that I first thought Gran was joking, but I soon realised that she wasn't. Now to me, Grandpa, she was the victim of 'spin'. Would you agree?"

"Totally … totally," came Grandpa's enthusiastic reply.

"You mean it's not your view, Gramps? And you think she is the victim of spin?"

"Yes, to both. Your grandma is another story, but the live-animal trade is like a disease. We caught it back when shipping became cheap as a result of too many ships being built. Believe it or not, this ship-building came directly or indirectly from the extraordinarily huge amount of money that was printed and loaned out by the USA, beginning at the time of the end of the Vietnam war.

"It's as if the world choked on the excess dollars and, suddenly, it was no longer the same world.

"Manufacturing goods cheaper abroad, in poorer countries, and dragging container loads of products around the planet to wealthier countries, became the basis of the new business model.

"Only now are people seeing the real damage that results from printing too much money.

"We've had the recent financial crisis in the US, the European currency cannot survive the loss of jobs to the Far East, and the US owes so much to China that each cannot do without the other. Add the threat of credit defaults in Italy and Greece and some South American countries and you quickly realise that things are more dysfunctional than anyone thought.

"And why is this so? You would want to say greed, but the truth is that it's caused by ignorance. And don't get me started on why that is. We'd be sitting here in the ute for bloody ever."

There was silence for a while.

Jamie was impressed with what his grandfather had said. Most of it he already sort of knew, and it fitted in well with his and his friends' world view.

Grandpa's description of the financial causes of the current situation were new to Jamie, however, and he made a mental note to research it fully once he was back at uni.

And did grandpa really say "bloody"? Wow! He'd never before heard him utter a swear word of any kind.

"Grandpa, it seems to me that a lot of the problem relates to over-production. Do you agree?" asked Jamie.

"A phrase we've all grown used to hearing and never question is 'economy of scale'. In other words, the belief that being able to produce a lot more of something leads to each individual item costing less, suggesting that we must all benefit.

"There is something innately wrong with the concept which takes a bit of explaining. It seems to make sense but in reality, if judged from the perspective of the 'common good', it is a disaster.

"It makes sense for a few things but not everything. It's mostly an excuse to make money. One day we'll talk through the arguments. That's if I can remember, of course," Grandpa laughed.

"You just suggested in what you said, Grandpa, that you don't agree with sending livestock abroad. How come you're planning to do so, and is this the first lot?" Jamie asked

"It is the first lot, and we have yet to confirm it with the agent. Grandma met some women friends for a shopping trip to Portland a couple of months back. The husband of one of them is an export agent and when the girls popped into his office for his wife to leave a message, your Grandmother mentioned we were on the land and it wasn't long before he phoned and made an appointment.

"Over tea and cake he made everything sound so simple. And when I asked about conditions on the ship, he pulled out his folder of photos taken on one of the boats showing animals being well fed and watered, and generally cared for.

"It all seemed pretty good. And when I asked about what happened at the other end, he produced more pictures of the inside of an abattoir in Kuwait or somewhere, which looked much the same as any abattoir here.

"And then, of course, there is the money. We don't get a lot, but in a drought situation like this, when we cannot run stock through till spring and fatten them for the local market, they have to go, regardless."

"And if sending the stock away by boat wasn't an option, Grandpa, what would you do?" Jamie asked.

"The simple answer is dig a pit for the bodies and shoot them. It's the last thing in the world a farmer wants to do but, if there is no water or rain, there is no other option.

"I've seen it done once on a neighbour's place, and awful though it sounds, I was impressed at how well the farmer handled it.

"Now that I've had time to think about things and since we've heard–and I think we can believe it–about the mistreatment of animals in some overseas countries, I'm of a mind that shooting the animals we can no longer feed is the better option. A quick death at home against a bloody awful trip abroad and the possibility of a cruel and painful end.

"The options are limited but I know which one I'd choose."

Jamie drove slowly around the end of the dam, not wanting to frighten the kangaroo. To his surprise, she was nowhere to be seen. What surprised him more was that the 'roo's baby had gone also. Jamie turned and looked at his grandfather.

"What's happened to the joey, Grandpa? I'm sure it was dead."

"It was, lad. And if you cast your eye way over there you'll see it, or what's left of it."

Jamie turned and looked towards where his grandfather was pointing. Out in the orange dust of the paddock, two wedge-tailed eagles were feeding on something brown.

"They must be young birds. They would have been a bit nervous, and waited until she had come out of the dam before they took it.

"Looks like she's headed off, probably into the trees. I reckon we should leave the water here in case she comes back. She should smell it, especially if we leave a bit of food nearby."

Jamie filled the plastic water trough with the water.

"There's a couple of heavy rocks in the back of the ute. Best put those in too. They should help stop it getting tipped over if she accidentally kicks it."

When they headed off, his grandfather asked Jamie to keep driving parallel to the line of trees. When they came to where the casuarinas finished and a group of ancient red gums clumped beside a creek, Grandpa asked him to stop.

The two men left the ute and wandered casually towards the gum trees.

"What are we looking at over here, Gramps?"

"Well, Jamie, I've been thinking through what we've just talked about. I've known all along that shipping live animals was a bad idea and it shouldn't happen and I have to start doing something about it now if we are ever to make a difference. I'm looking for a quiet spot where the digging is easy for the scoop on the tractor. We will need more than one trench of course so I will look around the property over the next few weeks.

"We're not sending those sheep away after all. I've decided they will die here. No fuss, no loading and unloading. It makes sense, don't you think, lad?"

Jamie smiled a broad smile at his grandfather. "Yes, Gramps, I certainly do."

On the drive back to the farmhouse, the two were quiet. Then Grandpa asked Jamie if he would consider being there to help when the time came to kill the sheep.

"Sure, Gramps, and if it's okay with you, I'll bring a couple of friends."

"It's going to take a bit of organising, lad. And the job itself will take time. We definitely won't be rushing it. I want to set an example to others who might also decide to face up to the truth.

"We've got to get it right. Things like killing in small batches and checking each kill was successful before burying. And I reckon we should kill from the back of the race–not the front–so that a beast doesn't see what is happening to the one ahead of it.

"The situation demands we put as much thought as we can into it beforehand and I'd appreciate your help, Jamie. You're a smart lad and you know a lot about all sorts of things and if you can get like-minded people interested, all the better. Now the only problem is how to tell your Gran."

Jamie was already thinking about it. He could see a late-into-the-night group discussion with his friends looming. Something to really get our teeth into, he mused. Maybe a video would be in order; strict rules about filming and internet access, though. For a moment he thought about adding links to sympathetic videos, then pulled himself up. That stuff would happen without him needing to do it. Forget the spin.

Let the facts speak for the themselves. Grandpa would want that.

Dinner at his grandparents' farm was always a delight and Jamie enjoyed helping in the kitchen.

Often Grandpa would join in, peeling the potatoes or shelling peas. There was a time, before his accident, when he would have kept working out in the shed or yards until

Grandma called him in for dinner by banging on the metal bin lid that hung from the veranda roof outside the scullery.

Preparing the evening meal was a time when all three were actively doing something together and it reminded Jamie of being at school camp or down at the beach house with his family on summer holidays.

People working together usually joked and sometimes said silly things to or about one another that they would not otherwise have said if they were simply sitting having a meal or a cup of tea.

His grandparents could never resist at least one or two digs at the grandson's vegetarian diet.

"What's the vego having tonight?" was Grandpa's favourite, usually followed with something like, "There is a new batch of lucerne pellets in the barn if you'd like to try them, Jamie? I knew you were coming so I ordered the ones with the extra mineral supplements and double molasses."

And when the laughter died down, Grandma would say something in Jamie's defence.

"Never having had a chop in his mouth hasn't stopped him growing and I reckon he's probably bigger and stronger than you were at that age, Mr Universe. And your hero, Cliffy, the sixty-one-year-old potato farmer who won the Sydney to Melbourne race, was a vegetarian."

At dinner, the conversation would most often be about the family, or the farm, or about what Jamie would do when he finished his studies. Tonight, in the middle of the first course, Grandma dropped a bombshell.

"I am now of the opinion that we should not send our sheep overseas," Grandma announced suddenly.

"While I think it's a very worthwhile cause, the truth is we can't afford the water," she continued.

Grandpa sat with a piece of lamb impaled on his fork,

halfway between the plate and his mouth, staring at his wife. Then he looked at Jamie and raised one eyebrow.

"Is that right, dear?"

"Yes, I heard it on the radio this morning. A listener rang in and said how, what with the drought and the problems with the environment, we shouldn't keep sending our water overseas."

Jamie and his grandfather exchanged glances.

"They made the very good point that our bodies are more than ninety per cent water and sheep and cattle are the same. I've forgotten how much water they said was contained in wheat, but it was also a lot, so we shouldn't send that away either. It makes sense when you think about it, doesn't it?

"Then they said if everyone stopped sending produce from one country to another, people would stop going on about that silly climate change. They said it wasn't the–what did he say–CFCs or the CO_2s that the scientists keep talking about, it was all that water going to where it wasn't supposed to be — strawberries from Africa to Aberdeen or oranges from California to Canada, and so on."

Grandma fell silent and continued eating, emptying her plate with the last mouthful of mashed potato.

Then she said, looking at her husband, "I'd suggest we don't send our sheep away George. I've gone off the idea totally."

Jamie and his grandfather looked at each other and then at Grandma. After a few moments, Grandpa spoke.

"Well, Mary, I don't believe they should be sent away either, so I'll ring and cancel their holiday trip with the shipping agent first thing in the morning."

Grandpa beamed a relieved smile at Jamie.

Grandma smiled, then said, "Thank you dear. Now, who's for fruit salad and ice-cream?"

8

INNER CITY SATURDAY NIGHT

The row outside got worse. It was midnight on a Saturday night in inner-city Melbourne. The gentle rain on the roof of the small upstairs bedroom would usually be a comforting sound and we would have settled into the warm bed and a deep and enjoyable sleep. But not on Saturdays. Not recently, anyway.

For the past five Saturdays, we had been woken in the early hours by our mystery neighbour.

Dave was in his mid-thirties and we called him the mystery man because we couldn't put a label on him, an occupation label that is. A person doesn't need to have a label of course, but certain people just invite the question: "What does that bloke do?"

Dave was one of those people.

Sound was amplified in these tiny back streets and through the little square backyards of the narrow cottages.

Dave lived with his mother Shirley and an old terrier called Butch.

When the terrier wasn't barking at nothing in particular, it was whining because it was cold, for it had nothing to sit or lie on in the all-concrete backyard when Shirley locked it outside and went down the street to shop or meet the girls–other older women she'd grown up with in Fitzroy–for an afternoon drink at the Royal Derby.

When Shirley got home, she talked loudly to Butch mainly about how much she loved him and had missed him that afternoon, and when Dave got home he shouted at both of them, telling them what useless bastards they were.

Most nights, Dave went out and things would quieten down. Shirley would watch the telly with the volume switched up, naturally, but then, thankfully, she switched it off and went to bed early.

Dave was big, footballer-like. He took a lot of trouble over his appearance. He was always shaved and his hair was perfect. He wore a suit during the day and smart casual clothes at night. But this almost impeccable image just did not fit the man.

Dave was arrogant, he swaggered when he walked, he shouted, and he bullied young kids in the street if they came too close to him with their bikes. And you couldn't help thinking that, underneath it all, he was probably a coward. Who else but a coward would shout constantly at his mother? He was a man you'd simply choose to avoid, someone you wouldn't want to know.

But there was more to consider than Dave's behaviour and dress.

Each morning at around 9.30, a large white late-model sedan would pull up outside number 107. The driver would double toot, then sit with the motor running until Dave appeared, usually with a piece of toast held tightly between his teeth.

Dave would jump in beside the driver and the car would

leave a little bit of rubber on the road as it took off to who knows where.

And then there were the golf clubs. At least once or twice a month, Dave would appear with toast as usual but with a fully loaded golf bag hanging from his shoulder. This he bundled into the boot, which opened as if by magic just as he aimed the bag at the back of the car. Then he would slam down the lid and dash for the passenger door as if the driver were about to leave without him.

But where was Dave off to? What did this man do?

Saturday nights turned bad when Dave got a girlfriend.

He would bring her home in the early hours. They would take the short cut from the pub along the lane that ran between our house and the shoe factory.

Well before they reached the street and turned the corner to walk the five metres to his mum's door, Dave and Ms X (we never did discover her name) would be screaming at each other.

It sounded just dreadful, violent. And although it was probably only minutes before they passed our window and turned into the street, the stark and horrible sounds of these two seemingly about to do each other serious injury left one wide awake and emotionally disturbed and unable to get back to sleep for a long time.

We discovered that a slab of cheese on toast and a cocoa helped to settle us down after these episodes, and we reminded ourselves that, bad as it was, it wasn't the London Blitz, and bombs would probably not fall on the house and for that reason it was now safe to go back to bed.

Being prisoners of this weekly event was beginning to bother us permanently. Not knowing how long it was likely to go on for, was depressing.

How could one possibly look forward to a pleasant weekend at home?

There were, however, not a lot of options.

We, like a number of our friends who had bought houses in the early 1970s in what until recently had been exclusively inner-city poor, and working-class suburbs, were very aware of the bad feeling being expressed by some of the local residents. Trendies and hippies were clearly not welcome here. These people belonged somewhere else, not here in true-blue battler territory.

Calling the police was not really an option.

For a start, you had to wait for Dave and Ms X to arrive, then try to get a constable on the scene before they'd moved round the corner. Too hard. And talking to an aggressive person who was also drunk seemed pointless.

Visiting Dave at home during the week for a friendly chat was the only civilised option, and I kept putting that off.

Tonight was the last straw.

We had jokingly thought that because of the rain, tonight might be different, but it wasn't.

We heard them coming, the sounds of the worst human condition after murder, torture and war. A drunken man and woman, neither of whom might ever have experienced love. And both most likely having grown up with alcohol-induced violence.

When the couple arrived below our first floor window the yelling stopped unexpectedly, but the sound that came in its place was more chilling than I could have imagined from my comfortable bed.

Instantly I knew that Dave had Ms X by the throat. A gargling, gasping sound, a thud against the brick wall, and then Dave's awful voice, "You fucking bitch! I told ya, you fucking bitch. Didn't I? I told you to shut up or I'd shut you up for good. So, bitch! How does this feel?"

Without thinking or listening I flew to the window, threw up the sash and hung out high above the couple. She had dropped to the ground and Dave had already landed his first kick.

"You're a fucking animal, Dave!" I called out, slightly surprised by the unfamiliar tone of my loud voice.

"Get off her. Be a bloody man for Christ sake, not a Moron. Get away from her."

I quickly ran out of things to say that I thought might make the difference. The next move must be more serious and I must not hesitate to do what seemed necessary, and to heck with the consequences.

Dave stopped and stood swaying, looking around to see where the voice had come from. Had he even heard what I said?

All this took only a split second. I saw the woman roll to one side and jump to her feet.

Faster than I could have imagined, she lifted her head and looked up to where she knew I must be in the darkness above. Then, in a voice from Hell she called out,.

"Don't call my boyfriend a moron you trendy bastard. Pull ya fucking head back in before we break it open along with ya fucking windows. And you and ya la-de-da slut can go back to where you fucking came from and leave us in peace. Fucking bastards, all of youse!"

And with that, she took the still swaying and confused Dave by the arm and dragged him away and around the corner.

I felt very strange. I was upset, confused by the outcome, and relieved that they had gone.

Had this been something I just hadn't understood? Is it

possible they were two professional actors discovering that they had the same sexual fantasy which they now played out every Saturday night? Act 1: eyes meet across a crowded bar. Act 2: a violent pursuit around dark alleyways. Act 3: well, that's their business. Don't be silly. Could Dave and Ms X be actors? No, and stop trying to rewrite the plot for God's sake. Be real.

Whatever the circumstances, I was determined to find some answer to what was now very definitely "the Saturday-night problem". I refused to consider staying the night elsewhere.

Unlikely as it may sound, the Gods decided to intervene.

Whether Dave split up with Ms X or whether on Saturdays they did something different, or came home by another route, I don't know. But from that night on, Saturday nights were given back to us, though we couldn't be sure they wouldn't turn up again.

Then one day, things changed for ever.

Butch died, then Shirley died a couple of weeks later.

Shortly after this, Dave came over to me in the street outside our front door one morning.

It was early. Not quite nine thirty, and no toast in his mouth.

He seemed a little disoriented, lost maybe. Shirley's demise had no doubt affected his life for the moment. I cruelly suspected he was now having to wake himself up, do his own ironing and the like, and that he no longer had someone to shove the toast into his mouth.

In a whining and grovelling voice I had not imagined he was capable of, Dave mumbled an apology for any trouble he might have caused us on his nights off when he said he sometimes had too much to drink. He said that now that Mum was gone he was going to live with his sister Gwen in Coburg, and that it was much better out there where people were not living in each other's pockets and one had a car port.

I really couldn't think of anything to say at that moment. I muttered "Best of luck, Dave." Then the white car pulled up and Dave grabbed a suitcase from the doorstep of 107 and threw it at the boot as the lid opened. In a flash he was in the white car; then it disappeared from our street for the last time.

'Shit,' I thought, 'I should have asked what the hell he did. Damn!'

The venue was Festival Hall a fortnight later. We were at a huge rally for the party faithful. A Labor government had been refused supply by the Senate. The Prime Minister had called for a new election. We were there in our thousands, young zealots, middle-class folk, left-wing intellectuals, and the blue-collar folk from the industrial heartlands.

What a night. Only the top men spoke. One of these was a senior union official, leader of the Australian Council of Trade Unions and destined in a few years to be a Labor Prime Minister.

When the prominent union leader had finished his speech, the crowd rose and applauded with great enthusiasm and only slowly was he able to back away from the microphone, waving with both hands and turning to left and right so that all could see him.

Suddenly, the curtains behind him parted and two big men in suits came slowly forward to escort the speaker back stage: his minders.

Each man took up a position on either side of their leader and each put a hand behind his shoulder to guide him safely while still soaking in the applause and waving continuously.

One of the men was our neighbour, Dave.

"Well, I'll be buggered," I said out loud, pointing to draw my partner's attention to Dave. "So that is what he does."

Together the three backed slowly to the curtains then disappeared.

All the bits came rushing together. Dave's immaculate dressing; the movie-style car rides; his remonstrating against little kids on bikes when he caught them riding on the footpath; the golf clubs; and then, the drinking and the violence.

In his own small way, Dave was a celebrity. He earned his daily toast watching over one of the most important men in the country. At work he bathed first in the light of his master's popularity and secondly in the hidden darkness of mindless ambition that surrounds all seats of power.

And then finally, Dave would go home to the tiny house where he lived with Shirley and Butch or, lately, to his sister's house in Coburg where there was a carport and where, I suspected, his sister Gwen now woke him up–maybe just a little earlier in the mornings–and ironed his shirts. And did Gwen make his toast?

Maybe I'll think Dave's story through again one day when I'm writing something that demands a minder, or a prime minister.

It's odd, but whenever I do think of Dave all these years later, I don't think of his job, only of the family dog Butch, whimpering on the cold concrete and the sad Shirley with her booze and the television turned up.

Maybe that's a clue to where the real darkness lies in everyone's life?

9

LOVE LOST

Kate noticed Jack and his mate Paul when she went down the street shopping for her mother some weeks before he and she first met.

Jack had driven to the town with the horse and dray from the road-building camp and was loading bags of potatoes in the lane beside Mrs Johansson's general store.

When Mrs Fleming's kelpie bitch–which she had told to stay with her neat little pony and trap parked below the pines on the foreshore–started lunging at the feet and tail of the heavy horse between the shafts of the dray, the big animal only put its ears back and stamped its front foot.

Then the dog aimed higher at the inner loose skin of the front right leg and attached its teeth to an exposed area of the softer hide, then discovered it could not let go.

At that point, the gelding threw up its back legs, kicking the dray and sending three bags of potatoes to the ground where they split open spreading potatoes over a large area of the lane.

Onlookers were aghast. But the tall young men with the horse and cart acted without panic or fear.

First taking a firm hold of the horse's bridle and speaking into its ear while stroking its neck and chest with his other hand, one of the men reached under the horse's belly and with a hand above and one below the dog's muzzle, pulled open the mouth and lifted the animal out and away from the leg and the horse.

With one hand holding both jaws together and the dog held tightly between his legs, he reached for a piece of rope hanging from the side of the dray, and quickly made a leash around the dog's neck.

The dog yelped as he let it go from between his legs.

Looking quickly back at the horse, which had its ears back and was snorting loudly, he called "Who-up Raj" in a strong but gentle voice. Then he turned towards the crowd gathered at the lane entrance to watch events and said, "Anybody own this kelpie?"

Mrs Fleming put up her hand. "I'm very sorry," she said. "The dog was supposed to stay with the trap until I came back from shopping. I do hope your horse is all right?"

The young man handed her the rope and dog and smiling said, "A nice dog madam, but better if it sticks to sheep I think. I'd tie it to your trap if I were you." Then he turned, looked quickly at the bite on the horse's leg, patted and praised the horse and went to help his workmate pick up the potatoes.

Kate had watched with great interest. She admired the young men as they worked loading the dray, and she was impressed with the tall young man's self-assured and pleasant manner.

She wondered if either of them ever visited her father's hotel. She certainly had never noticed them there.

. . .

It was a big day at the Grand Pacific Hotel on the Saturdays when the local cricket team played at home.

Kate and her older sister Anna were flat out helping their mother Rosa prepare meals in the kitchen and their father Darcy would often call for Anna to help in the bar when yet another large thirsty group walked in.

Kate wasn't allowed to do bar work. Her parents had decided that her sister Anna's sometimes over confident and flirtatious behaviour with men could have something to do with her being allowed to work behind the bar from a young age.

They thought she had received too much attention from customers who were pleasant and attentive to the impressionable young girl, constantly paying her compliments and commenting on her fine looks.

Her coquettish behaviour behind the bar would sometimes cause tension between her and her father. It was considered wise therefore, to confine Kate to work that was not constantly in the public eye, so Kate worked with Rosa in the kitchen and with the hired help, cleaning rooms and making beds.

Kate was happy with this arrangement. Most times she enjoyed working with her mother. Rosa would talk to her about all manner of things; things that Kate would probably never have learnt about if she worked in the bar. And she got to do the shopping, which took her away from the hotel and out walking.

Lorne played Deans Marsh at home the day Kate met Jack.

Jack and his friend Paul were not really pub blokes, but having a day off on such a fine day and with many of their friends involved with cricket, it was natural that they would visit the Grand Pacific. They stayed out on the lawns in front of the hotel and took turns to go into the pub for drinks.

Kate had just moved the second big pot of pea and ham soup off the heat to a spot where it would stay hot but not boil or burn when her father stuck his head through the door and called out, "Kate? Go and see if you can find empty glasses outside, would you love? We seem to be running out. Thanks."

Kate looked at Rosa, who nodded agreement. "Take the wooden tray with the better handles dear," she said, gesturing with her head towards the big sideboard near the back door.

When Kate wandered out into the afternoon sunlight she was surprised to see so many people. The outdoor tables were rarely fully used, but today they were all in use, and people who couldn't get a seat had found places to squat or lie down on the grassy patches away from the tables and chairs.

As she moved around collecting empty glasses, people who knew her from the town–shop people mostly–called out, "Hello Kate!"

A man's voice came from somewhere in the crowd yelling "Crikey! Where has she been hiding?"

She would have stopped and chatted to friends, but she knew that Darcy needed glasses in a hurry.

It was on her fourth foray with the tray that she spotted the two young men she had seen loading potatoes. They were lying on the grass along with three other fellows. They had not yet seen her approaching, and she was able to observe them for a moment.

Both were listening intently to one of the other men, a stem of grass in the older lad's mouth and a cricket ball in one hand of the fellow she guessed to be around her own age. Then the group all laughed, and the speaker's mate slapped him on the back as if to congratulate him on telling such a good story.

The younger man rose and tossed the ball to his mate, then collected the empty glasses. As he turned to head towards the bar entrance for drinks, he discovered Kate standing in front of him with her half-empty tray.

"Hello," he said with a big grin. Kate noticed that his ruddy face suddenly became redder.

"Hello," she replied. "Can I take those glasses for you?"

"Err … yes. Thank you," he replied, then, "Do you work here?"

Kate observed his open, boyish expression. He was not like many of the men who came to the hotel, just looking for a good time and hoping to meet a girl who would give it to them. They were the ones who would call out or try to get you to answer silly questions.

"Yes, I do," Kate replied. She instantly saw that he wasn't sure what to say, so she continued. "Didn't I see you loading potatoes at the store a couple of weeks back? You and your friend were having a bit of trouble with your horse and a kelpie."

The young man laughed and said, "You have a good memory and yes, that was me and I was with my friend Paul." He motioned towards the man lying on the grass behind him. "What is your name?"

"I'm Kate, Kate O'Malley. I live here with my family. My parents own the hotel. What's your name?"

"Jack Jones and I'm with the road gang. I look after the horses. Pleased to meet you, Kate."

A sudden voice from behind called. "Have you forgotten it's your shout Jack? We're getting thirsty over here."

Jack turned and called back, "Coming up." Then he

looked back at Kate and said, "Gotta go, Kate. I do hope we meet again soon though."

Jack's disarming smile prompted Kate to reply, "I hope so too, Jack, goodbye."

Jack came to town on Tuesdays and Fridays. His friend Paul usually came with him on Tuesdays when the bulkier and heavier supplies were collected from the store. It was also the day when machinery spare parts and other equipment arrived on the boat and were collected from the wharf by the two men.

When Jack came alone on Fridays, it was usually to top up supplies and collect the mail.

It was on a Friday that Jack bumped into Kate outside the store. Kate had a basket full of groceries on one arm and a bag with more shopping on the other.

"Hello Kate," said Jack.

"Hello Jack," Kate replied.

They smiled at each other, both unsure what to say next and both hoping the other would speak first.

Jack looked at Kate's shopping, then said quickly, "Can I carry the shopping home for you Kate? I've nothing to do except wait for the post and that won't get here for another hour at least. I was only going to take a walk along the foreshore."

"If you would like to, Jack. It's a bit of a hike up that hill. I wouldn't want to wear you out," she replied with a smile.

Jack noticed a twinkle in her eyes and laughed. "People are the same as horses. If they stand around too long with nothing to do, they quickly lose condition. You wouldn't wish that on a bloke, I'm sure."

Jack relieved Kate of her basket and bag, and they began to walk slowly towards the hill and the hotel.

They had taken only a few steps when Mrs Johansson came out from her store and called to Kate.

"Kate, you forgot the sugar, love."

She handed the bag of sugar to Kate, who thanked her and apologised.

"That's all right, Kate. It can happen to anyone." She paused and glanced at Jack. "Sometimes there are more important things to think about than a bag of sugar," Mrs Johansson laughed as she turned to go back into the store.

"Oh, and Jack, don't hurry back for the mailbag. I just remembered Jim said the post would be a bit late getting here today," and then she disappeared inside.

Jack and Kate stood smiling at each other for a moment, then turned and walked on. The two were quiet for a little while; then Kate said, "Do you have a family, Jack?"

Jack was quiet for a moment.

"Well, yes and no. My mother died just over a year ago and my dad when I was seven. I have a young brother, Alfred, who's fifteen. He lives in mum's old house with Mum's brother Jock in Colac. There were four of us, all boys. The older boys died in the war."

Jack fell silent. Then Kate looked across at him and said, "I'm so sorry, Jack. Losing your family so young. Gosh, it's hard to believe."

They were both quiet again.

Jack gave a little laugh and said, "I think Florence Johansson has become my mother now. She used to be quite grumpy with me when I first went into the store. Then Paul told her about my mum dying and suddenly she looks out for me as if she's taken on Mum's job.

"Spoils me a bit. Slips me an apple or a biscuit sometimes

when no one's watching. She can still get stroppy with me though. Always tells me off if I bring the cart too close to the front door. She's nervous with horses, I think.

But then Mum sometimes got stroppy with me too. It's funny how although they never met, Florence will often say the same sort of things, just like my mother would have said."

"Like what, Jack? What sort of things?"

"Well, a couple of times Mrs J has said exactly what Mum used to say to me, 'You'll see things differently when you grow up Jack.' Funny that, don't you think?"

Kate and Jack both laughed.

Kate told him first about her mother Rosa, then her father Darcy, and finally her older sister Anna.

"You must have noticed Anna, Jack. All the boys know Anna. She's very attractive."

Jack thought for a moment; then said, "Can't say that I have. Is she like you?"

Kate laughed. "Anna has blonde hair and is very petite. Dad jokes with mum that he couldn't have fathered two kids so different to look at, so whoever fathered the other one should chip in something towards her upkeep."

Kate told Jack how she mostly worked in the kitchen with Rosa and how sometimes they had to cook for fifty people when the hotel was booked out for weeks in summer and folk came from the city to enjoy the beach and surf.

It seemed they had hardly begun their conversation when, too soon, they reached the back door of the hotel kitchen. As Kate turned to take the shopping from Jack, the back door opened and Rosa stood looking at the two of them. Kate seemed flustered for a moment and then said, "Mum, this is Jack. He kindly offered to carry the shopping home for me."

Jack realised that he too felt a little uncomfortable, although he couldn't think why.

"… And Jack, this is my mother, Rosa."

Jack put down the basket and put out his hand and began, "Pleased to meet you Mrs … ," then realised he had forgotten Kate's surname.

"You can call me Rosa, Jack." Kate's mum shook Jack's hand warmly, then said to Kate, "We've got extra bookings for the weekend and they are arriving this afternoon so they will be here for dinner. We've got a big afternoon ahead of us love, so don't be too long.

"Just pop the bags over here, Jack. Thank you. It was nice to meet you. Maybe we'll see you again."

Rosa held open the door and indicated where Jack should put the groceries. Jack lowered the basket and bag onto the bench top and said goodbye.

Outside, Kate stood for a moment. She smiled warmly and said, "Thanks Jack. Might see you again next Friday morning if you're around. I usually go to the store between nine-thirty and ten. Take care. Goodbye."

When Jack got back to the store, Florence handed him the mailbag and smiled and said playfully, "You've had a busy morning, Jack."

Jack coloured up for the second time that day but managed to quickly think of an answer. He smiled sheepishly at Florence and then, looking away, said in an exaggerated voice, "Just part of growing up I suppose, Mrs J."

Florence immediately saw the joke and laughed loudly.

"You're a good lad, Jack."

They both laughed and said their good-byes.

"See you next week," Florence called as Jack took the mail-bag and the box of groceries he'd ordered earlier, and headed out across the road to the horse and dray.

.   .   .

Kate met Jack the following Friday morning at the store, and Jack again carried her shopping home to the hotel.

Excitement and happy expectation showed on both their faces when they met. Neither had been certain that the other would turn up. The fear of disappointment was dispelled the moment they saw each other. And Florence Johansson only just managed to hide her excitement at the two meeting in her store.

She busied herself and went off out the back so that they could be alone for a few moments. And when they left, she gave them each a chocolate biscuit from the jar beside the cash register, saying, "They will give you both extra energy to get up that hill."

As they began their walk in the sunshine and in view of the ocean, they were conscious only of each other.

Kate talked the most, though she tried very hard to appear relaxed and restrained or, as she saw it, "grown up".

She couldn't resist looking for little ways to tease Jack, to try to get him to show himself so that she could know him better, but very gently of course.

Then she became bolder and asked him more personal questions like–had he ever had a girl-friend, and if he had not, did he think he'd like to have one–to which Jack, not to be outsmarted, replied that, a man who spent as much time as he did with horses didn't need a girlfriend.

Kate instantly pulled a face and lightly punched his upper arm and said that was not a proper answer. Jack laughed and added, "Of course, I'm yet to find a horse that can cook, mind you, so maybe, one day when I finally get tired of my own cooking, I'll change my mind."

Kate did not respond and they were silent for a few steps, then in a quiet but deliberately affected voice, Kate announced, "No doubt you'll see things differently when you grow up Jack."

Jack laughed out loud and Kate began to giggle.

Jack attempted to chase her up the hill. Then, feigning exhaustion, he sat down on the bench seat that looked out over the sea. The seat marked the halfway point in the walk from the store to the hotel.

Kate came back and sat down beside him and they both stared out to sea.

When Jack regained his normal breathing he said, in his proper everyday voice and still looking out to sea, "I would like you to be my girlfriend, Kate."

Kate turned and looked at the side of Jack's face and saw, instead of the playful boy of a few minutes ago, the serious young man who could handle himself and a difficult horse, and a crazy dog and so much more. In that quiet moment Kate moved herself closer to Jack, then she put her arm through his and found his hand. She squeezed it gently and said, "I would very much like you to be my boyfriend, Jack."

She leant towards him and kissed his cheek, then rested her head on his shoulder.

When they parted at the kitchen door, they said very little. They felt the significance of the moment. They were in love and they were very happy.

"See you next week," said Jack.

"Be early if you can," Kate called as he headed off down the hill.

Jack turned and smiled back. "I will," he said.

Kate would always look out for Jack, and sometimes she would bring him something special from the hotel kitchen.

Sometimes she would laugh and tell him that he was too big for a normal wife to have to feed and look after, and he'd need to marry a girl who had experience in cooking big quantities of food, a girl who had maybe worked in the kitchen of a hotel, for instance.

Jack would laugh and ask where she thought a bloke would find such a girl, then she'd yell and box his ears.

Working on the roads meant Jack had time to think, and much of that thinking was about Kate and how he would have to prove himself to her father and show how dependable he was, and how he knew a lot more things than Mr O'Malley probably thought he did, and how he wanted one day to have his very own farm and a vehicle repair business and breed top quality working horses.

Jack knew a lot about horses.

At the camp, a new horse was always put under Jack's care for the first few weeks after its arrival. He'd get to know the horse, and quietly introduce it to the other horses and to its work responsibilities. He had a reputation for settling the more difficult young horses sent to work on the road, and the other men always came to him for help with their animals if something wasn't working out.

Although it seldom happened, when the horses were being put into harness in the early dawn and were sometimes standing too close together, one horse might lash out with one or both of its back feet or swing its neck and head around with its ears back and showing a mouthful of teeth to its neighbour or its handler.

Sometimes this would be a deliberate response to what it saw as a provocation by another horse that it didn't get on with and that it thought was getting too close.

Other times it could be because its handler was tightening a piece of harness too much or too quickly. Or maybe he had pinched the horse's tummy flesh while double-checking the tightness of the belly strap.

Jack was always close by and ready to help, giving a new

worker advice about his horse's temperament or settling a bad-tempered horse should the need occur.

Jack was very confident about his future, but for some reason he had this feeling down deep that Kate's father did not like him and, no matter what, would make their courtship as difficult as possible.

These feelings fell away whenever he was with Kate. Being with the one you love drives away a man's worst fears.

It was late May and almost two months since Kate's seventeenth birthday.

Jack went to Lorne earlier that week to pick up extra oats and chaff for the horses and other bits and pieces. Winter had arrived early, and the animals needed more oats each morning and night to keep them warm and working along the windy coastal cliff faces.

The town was quiet as Jack drove to the store and none of the lads came out as they often did when he pulled up.

It was cold and windy, and he couldn't blame them for not coming out.

When he went into the store the people working there, most of whom he knew, looked at him sort of funny if they looked at him at all. A couple nodded then quickly looked away. It felt strangely as though they did not know him.

When Jack went to the counter with his list of stores, no one came to serve him. Usually, at least one would say hello or yell out to ask how much road had been dug that week.

After a few minutes, Mrs Johansson appeared and did something she had never done before. She came around from behind the counter and stood in front of Jack and looked directly into his face. Then she reached out and took hold of his hand and in a slow firm voice said,

"Jack, there is something I have to tell you."

Jack felt confused. This sort of thing had never happened when he'd come to the store before. Mrs Johansson was silent for a moment, then she spoke.

"Jack! The O'Malleys have gone. They left in the middle of the night three days ago, and nobody knows where they went. People are saying that Darcy O'Malley had gotten heavily into debt gambling, and in desperation took the family and shot through. Kate's gone, Jack. I'm so sorry."

This story was recounted to the author by Jack Jones late in nineteen seventy. Jack's life story was the inspiration for the author's yet to be completed novel 'RESTLESS', a fictional saga portraying the lives of two young men growing up in Australia between 1900 and 1936.

FIND US

Publisher enquiries should include the full business name and address in all correspondence.

Email address:
admin@richardlee.biz

RICHARD LEE PUBLISHING

Fiction

Australian Short Stories by Richard Lee

ISBN - 978-0-909431-00-6

Restless: A novel about two young men growing up in Australia
between 1900 and 1936 by Richard Lee (Publication late 2022.)

Memoir

The Kite Makers: Six years of a child's war - Britain 1939-1945 by
Anita Sinclair.

ISBN - 978-0-909431-16-7

Out of Print Titles

Mathematics for Young Children by Helen Western

ISBN - 978-0-909431-01-3

Currajong: For Those Whom Schools Have Failed

by Bruce Wicking

ISBN - 978-0-909431-03-7

The Puppetry Handbook by Anita Sinclair

ISBN - 978-0-909431-04-4

Wordswork by Chris Davidson & Bruce Wicking

ISBN - 978-0-909431-06-8

Sheep Production by Murray Elliott

ISBN - 978-0-909431-07-5

Ducks for Starters: A Practical Guide to

Backyard Duck Keeping by Bruce Wicking

ISBN - 978-1-875207-00-8

Sweethearts - A novel by Colin Talbot

ISBN - 978-1-875207-02-2